Sinister Desire

WORKS BY SYK KELLY

CRUEL GODS SERIES:
BRINGER OF DEATH

CRUEL KINGDOMS SERIES:
SINISTER DESIRE

CRUEL KINGDOMS

SYK KELLY

Sinister Desire
Copyright ©
SYK Kelly, 2025
All rights reserved.
No part of this book may be used or reproduced in any manner whatsoever without written permission.
ISBN: 979-8-9924535-0-8

DEDICATION

For the little birds who desire more.

CONTENT WARNING

This is a dark romance novella containing the following trigger warnings: attempted sexual assault, physical assault, masks, stalking, kidnapping, some BDSM elements, CNC/dub-con, knife play, light bondage, off-page spousal abuse, off-page parental abuse, poison, murder.

SINISTER DESIRE

Chapter One

I was never one to care much for anniversaries or important dates, but as the ripe smell thickens with every hesitant step down the hallway, I'm reminded of how equally foul and sweet today is.

Three sharp knocks are the only warning I give before pushing the door, opening myself to all the problems it contains. Avoiding her wasn't an option this morning.

The sight doesn't surprise me. The room is always a mess, clothes in piles covering the floor, some hanging from the tall wooden bedpost, drawings scattered on the desk with crumpled papers by the waste bin— never in it. It's the smell of death hidden beneath the fruity perfume that almost takes me off my feet. My hand can't cover my nose quick enough to hide the odor as my throat convulses with a need to expel the apple I ate for breakfast.

A shiver runs up my spine as the kiss of the fall morning chill prickles my skin. I can only shake my head. It doesn't matter how many times I repeat myself to keep the window shut, how many times birds fly into the house, the insolent girl refuses to keep the damn window closed.

If I take a nail and hammer to every inch of the wood, my stepdaughter would break the glass just to spite me.

CRUEL KINGDOMS

"Up, Ember," I shout, picking up the clothes and tossing them in the empty basket tipped over in the corner.

Ember's short hair remains unmoved and splayed on the gray pillow.

When she showed up to breakfast one morning, smiling ear to ear as if she hadn't chopped away her beautiful, blonde locks, it was the day I was tempted to give in to her uncle Jack's requests to take her. It was that challenging smirk and tilt of her head while she waited for a tongue-lashing that gave away the game we played and will continue to play until she's mature enough to be on her own. Age be damned, I won't send her into the world unprepared.

"Ember! What is that smell?" Nothing on the surface looks to be the cause of such a wicked smell. How she can sleep through such a stench is beyond me. I have less than a minute left in this clutter before my body betrays me. "If you're hiding rats again, I'm—"

"What?" Ember groans with a lazy yawn. Her arms exaggerate a long stretch over her head. "Are you going to ground me, Audrey?"

Picking my battles with this girl is in my top five hardest experiences I've gone through and continue to go through. There is no real strategy with someone who likes to push boundaries, challenge everything, and play mind games. I can't deny that she keeps me alert and on my toes… and watching over my shoulder.

The bite mark on my leg throbs as a reminder that it could get worse.

It could always be worse; I remind myself of the same mantra I've repeated since I was a child.

If letting Ember have her rats keeps her from letting in stray dogs and cats, then rats it is. At least the rats have their own self-made cages and don't roam freely—yet. But I can't let her think I'm fine with it, or she'll up her game, so I tell her grounding would be the start of her punishment and leave it at that. Let her think about the possibilities in my bluff that I have no intention of following up on. Outside of grounding, what else is there to punish a teen with? She already has chores, hardly leaves the house, and never invites friends over.

"I didn't smell anything until you came in." Ember sits up with a narrowing grimace, waiting for my volley back, but my limit was met the moment I opened my eyes and knew what day it was.

"Breakfast is ready," I say, adding a sweetness to my tone that's slipping by the second. "It's your week for chores, so please hurry. We have a lot to do before the ball."

Ember lifts her already over-arched brow. "How are we going to the ball? We have no money since my father died, or have you forgotten?" Her hateful eyes travel down my silk dress and stop at the emerald necklace that sits just above my chest. The dress is one of the only items I've kept from my old, lavish life as a necessity to look presentable, but it's the emerald that I never take off. The one item I own that I would never part with; *It could be better.*

"We will all be at that ball," I promise more to myself. The glimmer in her blue eyes—the rare sight—melts the ice in my chest just a little. "I have a meeting in town to discuss the new dresses. Ally and Dee will be practicing their etiquette downstairs, so you'll want to start washing the floors upstairs until they're done." Separating my daughters from Ember wasn't something I ever imagined having to do, but this last year proved the three of them couldn't get along during the simplest of tasks. The separate classes cost more but are worth the lack of headache for everyone involved.

"Why don't you talk about him?" Ember looks ethereal looking out the window, with her soft pale skin and shining blonde hair, and when she turns, the sapphire daggers she sends my way are just as lethal—identical to her father in every way.

CRUEL KINGDOMS

"I don't know." *Lie.* If I could never speak about Richard again, it would be too soon. But I keep that thought to myself. I am a grieving widow, after all, and the last person who should see me openly loath my dead husband is the daughter he left behind.

I quickly slide my hand behind my back to hide the fact that it's now bare. I gave it a full year to rip the noose off. The weight, not only off my hand but off my shoulders, disappeared, forever gone from my life.

"Do you want to talk about him?"

"Not with you," she sneers and tosses her body so her back is to me.

Those words would have stung once. The girl was attached to that man, always at his side most hours of the day. His perfect little shadow.

"Happy Birthday, Ember." I shut the door before she could say anything else to press me.

All girls were difficult at some point, right? Alison had a nasty habit of saying no to anything I told her when she was four. Delany threw anything she could get her hands on just to see it shatter until she was five. Ember? Ember was just bloody difficult at all turns. Then again, she had reason to. Her mother died of a sudden sickness and was only with us for one year before her father had his accident.

We're her only family now, myself and her stepsisters. Her uncle Jack, on her mother's side, showed up twice to claim her when his gambling debts became too much, and his petty thievery landed him in jail more often than not. I don't care how difficult Ember is; she's not going with that man. Not that she ever asks about him, but now that she's eighteen, I suppose that's no longer my choice.

If it takes locking her in the attic…

SINISTER DESIRE

I shake that thought away. I won't be like him—like *them*, but this girl has me on the verge of doing things I never imagined myself capable of.

Do I feel bad for giving her chores on her birthday? No. We all have responsibilities and things we don't want to do but must. Birthdays are just a reminder that we're a little closer to death—to rest. But not everyone shares that bleak thought, so I promise myself to stop by the bakery to get her a cake.

Before I set to town, I pull the note that was left on the doorstep from my dress. The very note that I've been anticipating for a year but didn't think would come again, assuming he'd forgotten about me.

With shaky hands, I read it over again:

Happy anniversary, little bird.
It's been a year of the freedom I promised you.
I've bid my time for your faux grievances and allowed you to reject my gifts.
Now, the game has begun.
You hide, I seek. The only place off limits is the fountain. If you go there, I'll consider it your forfeit and my win.
I'd hate to hurt you on your birthday.
-Your faithful follower

Chapter Two

The familiar scent of fresh bread fills my nose, but the gossipy chatter isn't as loud as usual. I can't focus. I know the horseshoes are clanking up and down the cobblestone streets, but I can't hear them clearly, with the soft hum muting everything and everyone around me.

This was always my favorite time of the week, listening to the commotions of everyone's daily lives. Problems that don't belong to me.

My *faithful follower* stole it.

His letter, the perfect cursive penmanship, is branded into my mind. It's been a year since I've heard from him. The notes started two years ago and were always short and simple: *I found you*, or *Never again*. One was just *Almost*. Toward the end, they started growing more specific: *The cage will open soon, little bird*, and *I can't wait to play with you again*.

I try to focus on the kids running from their parents, a shoe cobbler who kisses his wife goodbye before kissing his mistress hello, and a mother dropping bread on the dirty ground, wiping it on her dress, and handing it to her son as if nothing happened.

I know these people—they know me—yet any of them could be my stalker. The word *again* indicates I know them, but nothing in the letters has ever let on who they are.

SINISTER DESIRE

The promise of hurt doesn't stop me from perching myself on the fountain's edge and looking at every face a little closer. I've known plenty of hurt in my life, and still, every eye that lands on me hitches my breath and has me bringing my cloak a little tighter around my shoulders.

The letter isn't going to stop me from working. This is my livelihood, how I put food on my table and dress all three girls. As of late, it's how I plan to provide the best opportunity for them: a chance to go to the ball, to make connections, and maybe find a reasonable suitor so none of them find themselves with a life like I've fallen into.

"Audrey, here's the book you wanted to borrow." The short, plump woman with graying hair isn't beautiful, but she isn't plain-looking either. Her pale skin freckles across her cheeks and nose, and her eyes are so light they look beige, if not for the subtle streaks of blue and green. My eyes always find their way to the emerald ring on her right hand.

She's a widow too. Most of us are.

"Thank you, Mallory." I quickly snag the book and look over the leather cover as if intrigued. Seeing the dagger imprinted on the front, part of me is. Romantic books bore me to tears, but a good mystery makes my head spin and gut twist in the giddy way girls feel over fairytales. "I do hope this one has a better ending. The last one was rather dull and *long*."

"You'll find this one a tad longer, I'm afraid." Mallory offers her usual wink before leaving and making her way to the chapel with a bag full of more books.

This was our routine for close to a year since Mallory first approached me at this very fountain with a proposition. One I refused at first and never saw myself pursuing until a few weeks later when my dead husband's lawyer showed up to inform me that we had no money, but we were entitled to the house—or rather, Ember was, as his first heir.

CRUEL KINGDOMS

Unfortunately, having a roof over our heads, no matter how large or lavish, doesn't provide food on the table. Firing the servants was the hardest thing I've ever had to do, followed by relearning to cook and clean. I sold most of my silks and jewels and gave excuses to avoid parties but eventually found my way back to this fountain with Mallory.

I still hold a Lady title because of Richard's Lord status, but that means rubbish when you don't play the social games. I tried at first, but I became busy; the gossip was no longer important, the parties grew time-consuming, and after I accepted Mallory's offer, it became hard to look into the wives' faces knowing what their husbands were up to.

My hand catches the emerald around my neck, thinking of the life I could have had, of the boy who saved my life long ago without knowing it would cost him his. As little as it is, there's comfort in a small piece of tragedy. Like when someone dies, and everyone cherishes life a little more for a few days. It could always be worse, but it could always be better, too, even if those better days are long gone.

I scan the crowd when I feel eyes on me. Maybe I'm being paranoid, but it feels as if the air shifted. Like the hairs on the back of my neck are trying to warn me of a brewing peril. The fog looks a little thicker. The birds sound a little sharper.

The streets are still lively, but one woman catches my eye. A stranger. Her dark skin and white hair aren't of note, but her eyes are a milky white that belong to the blind. I would have remembered seeing her around before.

Her head snaps to me as if sensing me notice her. The air catches in my lungs when her hand raises, and her fingers wiggle a small wave. Right. At. Me.

I toss my head in every direction, but no one's near me. When I look back, she's no longer there. I look around again, trying to peer into alleys and storefront windows, but I find nothing.

SINISTER DESIRE

I'm not sure if I imagined her with my lack of sleep or if she actually vanished into thin air, but if she was real, I do know she can't possibly be my stalker. Stalkers aren't typically women, old, or blind. Even considering that thought puts a sliver of a smile on my face, though it shouldn't. He's still out there, possibly watching me disobey his one request.

I lift my chin high, smile wider, and drag my finger through the fountain's water, just in case he is. He doesn't get to tell me what to or not to do.

The feeling of being watched doesn't go away. If anything, it grows stronger as I open the book to where the bookmark is securely tucked into place, finding the location I need to be at in five minutes.

As I stand and hurry on my way, I notice a familiar piece of paper sticking from the back. My heart nearly falls out of my chest as I pull it out. This can't be what I think it is.

I can't stop, or I'll be late, but I do take one more look around, pick up my pace, and unfold the note.

You forfeit, little bird.

Chapter Three

"Stay still," the man huffs.

I do as I'm told because he's not one who likes having to repeat himself. My neck hurts from hanging off the table, but at least I don't have to look at him.

I want to suck in my breath as his teeth bite into my breasts, but I know if I do, they'll sink in deeper.

Dolls don't breathe.

I know him, of course. Most of these men are palace guards sworn into celibacy to focus on their oath to protect their King and royal family, but some of them are of the town, and even rarer are frequent travelers from nearby towns—like this man—but it's easier to see them all as faceless, no named transactions.

They aren't paying for what their wives or girlfriends can provide, so I usually walk out of these secret locations sore with bruised skin and a struck ego. That doesn't bother me. What I don't like is cuddling or calling them good boys, but whatever it takes to collect the money they willingly hand over for the hour.

This man isn't like most, where a few naughty words, twists, and tricks of the trade have them finishing on me within minutes. He makes dolls and likes his women the same. So, I hold my breath and let him bite my breasts as he works his carving knife handle in me with one hand and himself in the other. The grunts and jerking sounds give him away since I can't see him.

He's close.

"Do you want those dresses?" His question throws me off, and at first, I think it's a trick to get me to talk so he can hurt me. Another person in my life who likes to play mind games. Then I remember, he did see me purchase two of the dresses and admire the other two I'm saving for before we started.

Before I can answer, he yanks the knife out and starts huffing heavily, like he's trying to hold his breath, too. When his grunts slow, I think he's done, but then his rough hand cups my chin and brings my head back to the table.

The mask is new. He wasn't wearing it when we started.

His dark eyes bore into mine, inches away, his head tilting to look at the red marks he made all over my chest. He lifts the bottom of his mask with one finger, enough to sink his teeth deeper into the prominent bite mark, and this time, I can't stop the hiss as my stomach burns the harder he bites.

The need to kick him off is strong, but my body knows better than my brain, staying unmoved even as he lifts me, so I'm sitting on the edge of the table.

I remember he asked me a question and nod quickly because the man doesn't like his dolls to talk.

When he corrects his mask and lifts his head, I get a better look at it. It's black wood, carved with intricate designs made imperfect by the deep scratches scattered about it. There are small slits for the eyes and a smaller one for the mouth. If this were anyone else, it would have been strange, but this man was as odd and particular as they come. I don't put it past him to want to be a doll like the wooden ones he carves and makes me play as.

There is something about it that makes my skin flush. I like the anonymity he's providing. The way he instantly becomes someone else behind it; that mystery I find so appealing in books coming to life.

I watch him as he lifts the red lipstick that's been waiting next to my leg. I already know what's coming, and although it doesn't hurt, it is hard to remove. He flicks the top off with his thumb and starts spreading it on my lips with a slow precision that drags the moment out longer than it needs to.

Although I've been naked in front of him a handful of times, and he was just using my body not five minutes ago, a prickle of insecurity hangs over me. I never paid much attention to his clothes, my head is usually hanging off the table, but I see them now. While I'm in nothing but the lipstick he's painting on me, he's tailored in all black, making him appear as if he's risen from the depths of Hell to be my personal tormentor for the next fifteen remaining minutes. He feels like it, too. There's a dark ire radiating from him, a forced sense of control felt through the soft strokes along my lips.

My thighs instinctively clench together. He doesn't notice the movement or the fact that I hold my breath at the mistake, too focused on the doll he's perfecting. I wait for him to finish, but he doesn't rub the red stain into my cheeks as usual.

"Do you like being a doll?" His voice is deeper, distorted with the mask covering his mouth, and I find my stomach dipping at the sound.

I nod because he asked, but part of me internally flinches, expecting a bite or soft smack that doesn't come.

His head cocks as he places his hands on either side of me on the table while raking his eyes up and down my naked body. Normally, I would shudder at being under a gaze so intense, but my insides are quivering with confusion.

Again, I don't get to answer before his arm slides under me. The quick movement startles me, but I don't react because I'm not supposed to be human. The way he moves me is so effortless that I actually do feel like a doll in his arms. Arms that are bigger than I thought. All of him is bigger than I ever took notice of before.

He places me on the floor and positions me into the perfect sitting doll. Lifting my chin with his fingers, he orders with a voice that's used to giving them, "Open."

I do without hesitation—*with anticipation* that I'm not used to.

His fingers slide over my tongue, and I can't help but enjoy the sweet taste of them—vanilla.

The tips of his fingers hit the back of my throat, activating my gag reflexes. The intensity behind those eyes is telling me to learn quickly, but I swear they light up at the sound.

"Perfect, little… *doll*." Part of me delights at his praise and the dark feeling coursing through me right now. I'm scared, and it reminds me of my faithful follower. The anonymity of him and his recent threat. I know he saw me at the fountain; he knows he won the game I didn't agree to play, and I can only wonder what he thinks he can do that will hurt me. Does he really think he'll get the chance?

My fingers itch to rid myself of the throbbing between my legs. I don't. Not because I'm to be as still as possible but I don't let myself enjoy these appointments. They can have my body, but they won't get my pleasure, not the real one anyway.

I repeat the reminder in my head like a broken record when he frees himself. I've had this dollmaker before, but maybe I've never fully looked at him because as he replaces his fingers with what I can only describe as a weapon—a gift from God—between his legs, I choke before he's halfway in.

He doesn't move. He just stares down at me. It's the crinkle next to his eye that tells me he's grinning. My stomach twists into tiny knots, and I blush under his shameless stare. I don't know what is different about this man, but he's not giving me the sick, stomach-churning feeling he usually does or when he was using that carving knife on me.

Maybe masks are my own personal kink. I've never had one, but I'm more sure this is it the longer I look at him.

"It's the eyes that are the hardest to replicate." He retreats to the tip, fists my hair, and slams to the back of my throat.

I close my eyes and fist my palms, quickly opening back up and hoping that doesn't get me into trouble. His eyes tell me I made a mistake as he repeats the motion. This time, I keep them wide open and see as he lights up again at the sound of me choking on him.

"Good, *doll*." He pets my hair, gripping it back into his massive fist. "It's the emotions in them that he can't replicate. Like yours," he thrust in and out twice as his fingers trail the tear that falls down my cheek. "I can see the fear in them."

Try terror.

I swear I sense movement behind him, but I don't dare take my gaze from his. I need the money, and I'm already here. And I can't. I'm physically entranced in whatever dark void they possess.

He chuckles. For a second, I contemplate stopping. This man is acting strange, and it's disrupting my attempts to dissociate with every passing second. Not only are my senses heightened, but I don't like that I can feel myself getting more aroused the longer I stare up at him.

SINISTER DESIRE

"You heard of that harlot whose husband killed her and the guard she was fucking?" His thrusts slow as he talks, reveling in my confusion. Saliva drips down my chin as the sound of him taking my throat fills the darkened dress shop. "What they won't tell you is that two others also died in a similar fashion. They haven't released it to the public yet, but we have a serial killer in our town. One who is targeting harlots."

My pulse rises. I swear I can see the delight in his eyes as he tracks the fear in mine.

I know he said serial killer, but I'm stuck on his choice of *our* town. He must have moved here, but the alarms ringing in my head are telling me that's not the case.

"You aren't a doll," his voice lowers to a deep, angry melody. "Show me what *you* can do."

He stills, and as if that were a command in itself, I jump to work him, using every trick I know. I twirl my tongue around his crown and take him deep—as deep as I can. He wants to see it all, and I have to use my hands for him, using them to put on the best show of my life so this can be over.

There's been a dangerous aura in this room since I saw that mask. One that grew opaque the moment he mentioned the killings.

I don't know why I slow when his hand finds my hair again, but I do. He's not adding pressure, allowing me to choose the pace and depth. I make the mistake of lifting my eyes and see that his brown ones are glued on me.

That damn mask has me dragging my tongue from his base to his head, letting the saliva string between us as I pull my head back for the visual.

Do I think my life depends on this moment? I'm working him like it does.

CRUEL KINGDOMS

"Are you enjoying yourself?" he clears his throat, pausing like he wanted to say more but stopped himself. "Show me how much."

No. I don't nod. I don't shake my head. He won't take my pleasure from me. This is just a transaction, and I won't let myself feel anything more than that.

I keep working him, waiting for him to say, *"Dolls don't swallow,"* but he says the exact opposite as he pulses down my throat.

When he's done, he leans down and grips my chin, and I swear I can hear him smiling beneath that distressed mask the moment a gurgle comes behind him. My eyes fall to the lying man, splayed in a pool of blood with the carving knife sticking from his throat—the dollmaker.

"I won, little bird."

SINISTER DESIRE

Faithful Follower

I always win.

I knew Audrey would show at the fountain, I just didn't expect her to perch her ass on the edge and smile as she twirled her hand in the water, taunting me while searching every shadow and corner for her *faithful follower*.

That shadow of a smile told me everything I needed to know about how she faired this last year. My little bird might still be stuck in that damn cage, but she's grown wings *and* a backbone.

That's the only reason I don't regret making the decision to leave her be for a year. She needed to learn to stand for herself. To make decisions for herself. Control and choices aren't things Audrey is familiar with, and being taken care of, coddled, and told everything immediately was never going to familiarize her with the concepts.

Did I like knowing she was a harlot, fucking men, to provide for herself and her family? Absolutely not. Those days are almost over for her once she sees that I'm her only choice.

If she listened to my warnings about the serial killer, this should be her last encounter, but I know her too well to believe that. Audrey likes being scared, or rather, nervous. It's not the fear, it's the anticipation, the build-up.

I nod to Duke, my right-hand man, who's standing guard outside of the dress shop. He faces me, hands behind his back with a smirk that makes my eyes roll. My face doesn't need to give away what just happened behind that door for him to know. Duke could hear a mouse squeak behind the walls of a bakery.

I don't always win.

I pull the gold from my pocket and toss it to him before shoving him inside the dress shop to get to work.

"Not a word," I warn him, pointing to the dagger at my hip.

He chuckles silently and heads straight to the scene.

Hearing him boast about winning a bet I didn't care to make isn't on my list of things to do today. Neither was mouth fucking that defiant little minx, which is exactly why I'm down a gold coin.

Duke gets to work, cleaning away the blood puddled on the floor, not bothering with the body because he knows I like to take out the trash myself. We're swift and efficient from too many years of experience.

When I'm done wrapping the dead man with nearby fabric, I toss him over my shoulder. This man was going to die today regardless, but seeing the wince on my little bird's face while he was fucking her with the tool that's still plunged into his neck had me seeing red. He's lucky I didn't see the bitemarks first. I wouldn't have been so quick.

My head jerks back to the table, spotting the lipstick. I couldn't help myself when I saw it next to her. I had to paint the red over her plush lips, marveling at the memory of when I first saw her.

As much as I didn't want her as a still little doll, I saw the opportunity that so clearly presented itself and took it. Her mouth is a fucking blessing that makes me want to believe in God, and my blood is pumping to return the favor. I swear the taste of her is going to have me looking to the sky and humming hymns.

SINISTER DESIRE

I pocket the lipstick, dropping the note and gift on the table. She won't use the gold, too determined to provide for herself, but I want her to have the option if she needs it.

Everything with her needs to be slow. She's been a caged bird for too long and the first thing she'll do if she feels like she's being caged in again is fly away.

Not again.

She might not have agreed to play these games with me, but I sure as shit am going to have fun playing with her, and soon enough, she'll remember exactly who I am.

Chapter Four

Paranoia comes with being a harlot. Every time I leave a location, I'm eaten up with the thought that every person I pass knows what I did behind those doors.

Do I regret becoming a harlot? No. I don't regret many things in my life, and doing whatever it takes to provide for my family isn't one of them. I see a side of humanity that others rarely do, and as depraved as it sounds, I feel useful, sometimes dirty and defiled, but my life hasn't had much purpose besides pleasing the men in my life. Why not the rest of them, too?

As I walk down the fog-cloaked, cobblestone alley, my ears are ringing, my paranoia is bordering hysteria, and my neck is hurting from looking over my shoulder every few minutes.

After my stalker forced me into the bathroom to clean up, I found that the dollmaker, the blood, and any sign that anyone was there, gone. All that was left was a familiar note and a bag of money.

I look forward to our next game.
-Your faithful follower

There was a folded paper beneath it, a cutout excerpt from tomorrow's paper that announced that, in light of the recent murders, the ball is going to be exclusively ticketed. With the precious prince's return from his decade-long military career to find a bride, the King is taking extra precautions.

Of course he knows I want to attend the ball, everyone in town does, but it feels like a bigger message, another game that I'm not privy to yet.

The amount for one ticket is more than I can save in a year, and with the amount of gold in the bag, I doubt it's the dollmakers. My stalker knows me well enough to know I won't use his money or gifts, which is why he didn't specify whose it was in the letter.

My stomach turns as guilt slams into my chest. I didn't know the dollmaker well, but he didn't deserve to die.

He wasn't the first dead body I've seen, but his death isn't tilting my world upside down or leaving me sobbing and praying that I follow after him. My fingers find the emerald around my neck for the tenth time today. I can still smell his burning flesh and see his crisped, charcoaled skin before me, but even more, I can hear his soft snickers and low whistles. I can see his cold glare that warmed after only a week of hiding out together. Charming, that's what I used to call him, because he was anything but.

I push the memories away to focus. It was just a nightmare, I tell myself, reworking the day in my head, imagining how today should have gone: I simply walked into the dress shop, looked around for a while, and placed my order. I don't even know a dollmaker.

I repeat the phrase again, straightening myself as I approach the baker's counter, living off the spices in the air, two of them more distinct than the rest: cinnamon and rosemary. A second of serene peace passes over me.

"Audrey," the old baker says my name like a distant name he can hardly remember. "I haven't seen you in some time." He shakes his head with correction. "I see you at the fountain, around town, but I don't see you here. I assumed you would have had those two bring your order to the house." He motioned to the arguing teens in the corner. "Lucy! Brock!

CRUEL KINGDOMS

Enough bickering in front of customers. Get Lady Audrey's order from the back."

Lucy stops braiding her black hair to eye me suspiciously, her head snapping away to look around for the girls. She and the twins had been in the same circles until Lucy broke her arm in our garden a few months ago. "Ember's birthday?" she asks with a shaky breath.

I offer a smile and nod. "Eighteen today. You're not far behind, right?"

"She's sixteen." Brock steps between us, shielding her from me. He wasn't her brother, but he was definitely like one. The twins told me all about how Brock hovers around the girl, baring his teeth at anyone who looks at her wrong. It doesn't bother me so long as his teeth baring and fists aren't on my girls or Lucy, which doesn't seem to be the case. His and Lucy's arguing never gave me pause either. Their kind of arguing reminds me of the butterfly fluttering in your stomach type of bickering. The egging each other on until you're both laughing and forgetting what you were even talking about kind of banter.

"Right. Same as the twins," I say. "I know they miss having you around. Both of you. You should stop by sometime."

I witness firsthand what the girls mean by baring teeth. The boy is nearly snarling as he glares at me. "If Ember is still in that house, we're not going."

Lucy's arm flinches as she folds them against her chest, looking up at him with unabashed gratitude. A sting of jealousy strikes me. A cruel feeling that quickly turns into my own sense of admiration and relief that she has someone to protect her when I didn't.

The baker barks for them to hurry before disappearing to the back himself. I heard Lucy telling the girls that he bakes himself two extra cakes to nibble on throughout the day, which shows in his rounded belly and cake-crumbled beard.

SINISTER DESIRE

"Maybe they can meet you here then?" I suggest. I'm not surprised to hear she doesn't favor Ember when all that girl does is challenge everyone around her. It was the girls who were heartbroken when Lucy stopped all contact after the incident.

Lucy's eyes soften as she nods. "Yeah. You can tell them to come by next time. Just not Ember, please."

I don't pry because I can see the signs of someone who is holding onto something they rather not talk about. Not that I could with them rushing to the back to grab my order.

Brock returns and drops it on the counter with an assessing, judgmental glance over. When I thank him, he gives me a curt nod and disappears to the back.

Before I leave, I peek inside and sigh in relief. For once, a piece of my day doesn't involve a letter.

"Wait!" Brock runs toward me with a smaller box. "The second order came later, so I forgot about it."

This time, my insides are shaking as much as my hands as I open the note sitting on top, using my teeth to help.

Save me a bite?

Chapter Five

I'm not through the door when I hear screams echoing down the hall. As quickly as I can, I drop the boxes on the counter and rush toward the chaos.

"You did it on purpose!" Ally's shriek is laced with agony as her cry catches in her throat.

"You're evil!" Dee yells. "The spawn of Lucifer himself!"

I can't run fast enough. Dee's the calm one of my two girls. If she's yelling, then whatever Ember did was something worse than ever before. I want to call out, but I hold my tongue to catch them off guard.

This home once offered every luxury and comfort one could possibly want, but right now I find it hard to admire a home that doesn't allow me to get to my daughters fast enough. The kitchen island is now pointless and in the way; the dining room is now too long, and the moody chandeliers are casting light that blinds me as I push through yet another door that doesn't contain them. It's when I finally reach the entryway that I find them.

I'm happy I didn't announce myself. If I had, I wouldn't get to witness Ember's delighted smirk as she looks down at Ally, who is cradling her ankle with tears streaming down her face. Dee holds her from behind, glaring spears of fire at her stepsister.

SINISTER DESIRE

"Mom, she mopped the floors on purpose!" Ally sniffles with a deep sob. "She knew we were practicing our steps!"

On cue, Ember's face softens apologetically, morphing into a completely different person. Strangely, it reminds me of the dollmaker's dolls, the wide eyes and perfectly placed smile. "It was my turn to do chores. I only did what Audrey told me to. On my birthday, I should add."

"You were to do them after we practiced!" Dee cranes her arm back and throws her shoe, her black hair swings into her plum face at the strength she puts behind it.

Thankfully, she misses Ember. One injury at a time.

"Ember," I sigh a heavy breath, my heart slowly cracking away seeing Ally's plum, tear-streaked cheeks. With a softness, I don't mean, I tell Ember, "Please go to your room."

Without my yelling or loss of temper, Ember doesn't get what she wants. Pouting, she tosses her hair before stomping up the marble stairs. "Your hair is a mess, by the way," she yells back.

"Why are you so nice to her? She's evil. She mopped these floors, knowing we had etiquette class. The teacher even left because she can't stand to be around her when she does things like this. Last week she—"

"Put glass in your slippers. I know." I shake my head and temper the rising fury, remembering how Dee almost severed her toe. "But she lost her father." I quickly correct myself. "You all did, but she lost her mother, too. Antagonizing her only makes things worse. Sometimes, as much as we don't want to, we have to ignore people and pray they go away. In the end, evildoers always get what they deserve."

The same can't be said for my faithful follower. He isn't like the other men in my life, where if I make myself unseen, they forget I exist. I thought he was, but I know better now. He'll be back. The more I ignore him and his gifts, the more he'll send them, and now that he's made himself seen…now that he's *killed* someone, I'm not sure I'll ever get out of his sights.

There is no going to the police because then I would have to explain why I didn't report the notes sooner. I would have to explain the murder of a man who paid me for sex, which is not only illegal but humiliating, not taking in the fact that there is no evidence to support my claims. No one is going to miss or notice the disappearance of a dollmaker who didn't live here.

If I believe the lie I tell my daughter, that evildoers get what they deserve, I'm positive my stalker returning into my life is a punishment sent for me. It hasn't even been a full day and my compulsion to check for another note has me pining after the door.

I take Dee's sharp chin between my fingers and tuck her dark hair behind her ears. "What do I always tell you?"

Her chest rises and falls quickly before letting out a long exhale. "When they want to take away my smile, lift it higher." *While keeping the knife hidden behind your back,* is what I didn't teach her. It's a lesson I learned too late in life, but they're still too young.

I lightly touch Ally's foot, and she cries out again. "I want to cut it off! It hurts so much! I think I'm going to throw up. What if it's infected? Mom—"

"Quit being dramatic," Dee rolls her eyes.

They aren't identical twins, and neither are their personalities. Ally is a bit of a drama queen who dreams of fairytales, while Dee is the realist between them. Delany got her father's raven hair and dark eyes, while Alison got my mother's auburn hair and my green eyes. The only traits they share are their father's dimples.

SINISTER DESIRE

"I'll call the doctor. Don't move."

Another bill at the worst possible timing. So long as they send Dr. Douglas, I have ways that will put his house visit sheet to the wind.

A broken leg.

I had to feign a dizzy spell that would give Dr. Douglas an excuse to escort me to my room for twenty minutes. He's my patient now. A grabby one.

It didn't shock me when he pulled out the nurse uniform, already knowing what this visit would come to.

I could use the gold to pay, but then I would be indebted to my stalker, and I won't let another man own me like that ever again. This is easier, and with strings that I'm aware of.

Internally, I'm already adding up the money I have saved with the amount I have promised from the rest of the names, hoping it's enough to purchase the rest of the dresses. The tickets I'll worry about later. There are a few guards on my list I can bribe.

"I wish you were blonde," Dr. Douglas says as I move on top of him. All of his real nurses are blonde. I run my hands through his graying hair and lead his head toward my exposed breasts. All men shut up when their mouths are busy.

By the time he's finished, I'm done recalculating our funds in my head again and planning this week's dinner. I'm still in the shower when I hear my door click closed. I'm sure I heard it lock too, but no one else has a key to my room to be able to do that. I wait ten more minutes in the hot steam before I step out, cursing, when I realize I left the towel on the bed.

CRUEL KINGDOMS

I don't make it two steps when the light burns out, painting the room completely black.

Not again. That's twice this month that I didn't notice how low the wick was.

Although I can't see anything, I know my bathroom enough to walk through it. It's the dripping water that makes it slippery and forces me to slow down before I have to call Dr. Douglas back.

The hairs on the back of my neck stand.

He's here.

I can feel him and his deranged aura. If I believed in witchcraft or superstitions, I would say it was his dark energy that forced the candle to burn out.

There's no point in hiding my naked body with my arms, so I don't bother. He had his eyeful while I had my mouthful only a few hours ago. I can still feel him, his phantom arms carrying me to the ground, his large hand on the back of my head.

"I know you're in here." My voice comes out in a weak whisper. If my skin wasn't already flush from the heated water, it would turn crimson from the flush that creeps up my neck and fills my cheeks.

There is no place for me to go. The door is three steps in front of me. Someone like him would expect me to go for it, to try to escape.

I try one step back.

My back meets something hard. His arm wraps around my waist, while the other hand wraps around my mouth, anticipating for me to scream, but I don't. I groan against it at my sorry attempt to struggle under his strong hold.

We shuffle forward a few steps. My feet slide on something warm and slick beneath me.

"I'm not going to hurt you, little bird." His voice is oddly reassuring, but I don't trust it. I don't trust him. I want to retaliate, but, as usual, my body doesn't agree with my mind, remaining stone still in his secured, cavernous hold. "I wasn't planning on coming in here this early, but I saw the carriage outside and got a glimpse of the end of your little show. Tell me…"

Knowing he was watching has my pulse rising. If anyone were to look at me, they wouldn't see it, but my insides are twisting with uncertainty and some certainty I hope isn't true.

His grip on my mouth tightens, dangerously close to covering my nose and cutting off my ability to breathe. With my body hanging uselessly against his, he walks us forward and flicks a match, relighting the candle and lamp I hardly use. The scene before me is exactly what I thought I would see and hoped I was wrong about.

Dr. Douglas lies unconscious in the corner of my washroom. His head's bleeding on the tile floor. His hands and feet are tied together, contorting him at an odd angle. The slight rise and fall of his chest is the only sign he's alive, but with how slow it's becoming, he won't be for long.

"Is this man your lover or a client?"

Since I can't talk, I shake my head. "Neither," I try to say against his palm.

"I'm going to uncover your mouth, but if you scream," his deep chuckle rattles my core. "You'll force me to resort to measures I'd rather not have to."

CRUEL KINGDOMS

Baffled isn't the right word to describe the perplexity of his threat. He murdered a man this morning and has another dying on my bathroom floor. What measures does he not want to take?

The dangerous muscles next to my ears and against my back are enough to get me to nod my head, letting him know I understand. I'm at his mercy with nothing but my teeth and nails as weapons; neither is a match for so much as one of his demanding glowers.

His hand leaves my mouth and I let out a breath that I didn't realize I was starving for. "Who is he to you?" There's a warning in his voice that's different than when we were in the dress shop. He was playing before, but that game is over, and I'm not sure this is the next one he started.

"He doesn't matter." If I could cross my arms, I would. I should be cowering and begging him not to hurt me, too, but something tells me he won't. He's had plenty of opportunity if he really wanted to.

A low, considering hum reverberates through him. "Then neither will his death?"

"He's a doctor!" I blurt out before he can think of moving to make that final blow. "I can't afford the bills. He lets me pay him in other ways." I tell him honestly because if I know anything, it's that he already knows the answer to the question he asked me. If he saw the end of the show, as he called it, then he also heard Dr. Douglas say he wanted two more sessions before his notes could disappear and I could consider myself paid in full.

My answer seems to please him because his hold loosens, and although I'm facing away, I can sense him grinning. It's in the way his distorted voice lightens. "If you're hurt, I can always stitch you up myself."

The breath is pulled from my lungs. The scar on my back tingles.

SINISTER DESIRE

"I'll give you a choice, little bird. If you choose right, he'll be the last to die tonight."

The air hasn't come back to my body to fully process what he just said or form any sort of question or argument for him.

He spins me around, bringing my front against his, gluing us together with only his shirt separating us. It's not until his hand lowers to the small of my back that I'm brought back to the present. To his thumb trailing my chin. I jerk my head to the side before I'm sucked in to the oddly erotic touch.

"You can't harm him. He's helping me." I know I sound like a child and I'm probably pouting, but I need Dr. Douglas' connection. It's hard to find someone who willingly bends the rules.

"He's helping himself." He takes a step back, leaving just enough room between us that I shudder as my nipples graze against his shirt. "He's using his status to take advantage of you."

"And you aren't?" I argue despite myself.

A thick, tensioned pause hangs between us. One that feels like a knife is hanging there, waiting for one of us to grab it first.

His ear drops to his shoulder. "Do you know what I do for a living?"

"Murder?"

He laughs again but doesn't confirm nor deny my accusation. "I would have thought you admired that part about me. Do you want to be the pot or the kettle?"

Black spots fill my vision in the already dark room, my mouth gaping. I take a step back, needing space from him and his words, but my foot slips on something slick beneath my feet. My bottom hits hard against the ground.

I don't dare take my eyes off him, watching as he offers me his hand. Another offering. I bat it away, seeing my palm painted red.

I chance one last look to the corner, and I know the second my eyes land on him, I'm watching the last rise and fall of Doctor Douglas' chest, blood spilling from a wound I can't see.

"You're not the only one who can't afford medical bills. Any man who uses his status to get something from you is fucking wrong. I don't care how you want to spin it to make yourself feel better." Everything about this man is screaming anger. From the drop in his shoulders to the way he's standing over me. My focus falls to the tightening of his fists.

I want to feel bad, but as I look back at the doctor's dead body, I realize that my stalker is right. The doctor *was* using his status to take advantage of me and likely others who were too poor to pay for proper care. While I saw our arrangement to my benefit, I've worked too hard and become too independent this last year to be taken advantage of.

Am I wrong for returning this dangerous man's anger back at him for making me realize how weak I've been rather than for killing someone on my washroom floor?

"What's the choice?"

He looks thrown off by my question until realization settles over him, and he dismissively says, "Shower," instantly straightening my back with the authority in his tone. The assurance he has can only come from experience commanding others, someone used to being in a position of power. I'm not sure what kind, but I'm positive he gives orders and doesn't take them.

SINISTER DESIRE

Without offering his hand again, he leans down to my level, his arms resting on his knees. The anticipation is thicker than the tension in this room, neither of us offering the other anything until he utters, "You're still not ready."

He stands, crosses his arms, and leans against the counter, nodding toward the shower in silent order before reminding me that I do have the choice to return downstairs covered in blood if I prefer.

"Not ready for what?" My body follows the command, turning the water on, testing it before stepping back into the steam. When I look down, I'm taken aback by how much blood is washing off me. If only I could see the weakness wash away with it.

I am not weak. Not anymore.

He doesn't answer me, and when I look where he was a minute ago, he's gone. There are no other noises as I finish scrubbing myself until I'm too sensitive to walk. When I step out this time, the room is just as clean as the dress shop. Not one spec of blood is left. It's as if nothing happened. I inhale, straightening my spine, *because nothing did*, I tell myself.

I'm not even in the kitchen before someone is knocking on the backdoor. The noise startles me enough that I jump, but I quickly regulate myself. As I make my way to the door, the repetition plays in my head: I don't know a dollmaker, and Dr. Douglas left thirty minutes ago. Nothing unusual happened today.

"Two dresses for a Lady Audrey." The man holds white boxes with pink bows out for me to take. He tips his hat to me, and I hold in my sigh as I offer him two coins, thank him, and shut the door. I put the order in this morning. They were fast.

CRUEL KINGDOMS

"What is that?"

I nearly drop the boxes at the intrusion. "Oh, Ember, you nearly gave me a heart attack."

"Pity." She shrugs. "What's in the boxes?"

Shit.

A loud, demanding knock at the door saves me. The last thing I need is Ember's opinions on my progress, or lack thereof after I promised we'd all be attending the ball.

When I open the door this time, the man in front of me sends me a year back in the past before my reality presses in. The police officer offers a curt nod, asking to come inside. My head spirals in too many directions as we motion through the pleasantries while I make a pot of tea, and we settle on the couch.

"What do we owe the pleasure, Officer Williams?" I don't grab the cup, knowing if I do my hands would shake, giving away my guilt. My ability to stay calm under pressure falters when it comes to certain men, and while this officer hasn't harmed me, he reeks of alcohol. If I weren't looking at him, I would think I was sitting in front of my father, smelling the same cheap whisky.

I don't know a dollmaker, and Dr. Douglas left thirty minutes ago.

"Please, Audrey, we've known each other long enough."

"Okay, *Mike*. Who died?" I bite my tongue. I can't believe I asked that out loud. I don't know why I asked that. It's just, the last he came to my house someone *had* died. I give an awkward giggle and internally promise to hang myself later.

SINISTER DESIRE

"You were in town today." It wasn't a question. "Seen by the fountain with a woman you're familiar with, Mallory?"

"Yes, she gave me a book to borrow." This isn't the line of questioning I had in mind. I hold my breath, waiting for the dollmaker, or the dress shop, or a mask to be introduced. I doubt he would ask about the doctor so fast, but I wait for that too.

"Can I see it?"

I nod and rush to grab the book from my room. The bookmark, gold, and notes were already safely locked away. As I pass the kitchen, I notice the cake box wide open and a scoop taken out as if someone had used their hands to grab it. The word *Happy* is scraped off, and a single burnt candle is stabbed through the center. The thing was for Ember, so I can't exactly yell at her for it. I know it wasn't my girls; they wouldn't dare use their hands for food.

Mike flips through the book as if there is something of significance. "Do you borrow books often?" he asks.

"Of course. She has a similar taste. Hopeless romantics, you can say. We exchange books weekly."

"I see. And after you borrowed the book today, where did you go?"

Shit. This was it.

"I put in a dress request, picked up a cake, and came home. My daughter broke her leg, so we called the doctor for a home call." I couldn't be more lucky that the dress boxes were on the counter as proof and reason I would enter the dress shop. "What is this about Mike?"

He finishes the tea, sets the cup on the table, and leans back with a curious look. "Mallory was found murdered. We can't release too many details, but I had to follow all the leads."

CRUEL KINGDOMS

His leads brought him to me?

I don't have to fake a dizzy spell this time. With my heartbeat ringing in my ears, my vision starts to spot for the second time today. "Mallory is dead?"

Could this have been my stalker? He murdered the dollmaker and the doctor. He told me harlots were being murdered. But why warn me if he was the murderer? I wait for more, sure he's seconds away from telling me about the dollmaker.

"I am sorry to have to tell you this. It seems I'm only the bearer of this kind of news to you." He moves his fingers to curl the ends of his mustache. It's exactly as he did a year ago, just as the same sinking terror clawed at my insides until he left. "Did you happen to talk about anything? Did she say anything about meeting with anyone later?"

"No." I cough to clear the lump in my throat, flattening the creases in my dress down my knee. "I'm sorry, no, she just gave me the book and left. Sometimes we talk about the last book, but she just left today. I think we were both too busy. Too many errands with the upcoming ball."

"Right." His smirk twitches in that judgmental way others do when they pity me. "If you think of anything, let me know, okay?"

"How was she killed?" I can't stop myself from asking. I need to know.

Mike bows his head and when he lifts it, his forehead creases with a somber frown. "The papers are reprinting as we speak to get the news out sooner, so I might as well tell you. We think we have a serial killer, Lady Audrey. One who is targeting harlots. All six so far have had the same poison in their system and cut across their necks. Their money and jewelry were stolen from their body." He watches as my face falls in horror. Seemingly pleased with my reaction, he excuses himself, again telling me to call him if I come to know anything.

"Of course." I thank him out of politeness because I'm sure not grateful for the news like I was a year ago when he told me my husband had been in an accident.

Chapter Six

After the girls go to bed, I sit in the dining room with the small box of cake. The one my stalker left me. It wasn't a cake at all, but pumpkin bread with thick vanilla frosting. My favorite.

I'm brought back to the pumpkin patch Charming found me in, my breath labored from the strawberry juice that was still fresh on the knife that had cut my back. Even dying from the allergic reaction and covered in blood, I smiled when I saw him. He was the most hauntingly beautiful person I'd ever laid eyes on, so much so that I thought he was an angel appearing to greet me before I died. When I woke two days later, I'd been cleaned and stitched up with him glaring at me with those dark, cold eyes. That was the second time I smiled at him.

The problem is he's the only one who knew my favorite cake, and he's been dead for sixteen years. If there was a possibility he was alive, I would consider that maybe he was my stalker, but I watched his body burn before my very eyes. I've never told anyone about him or talked about myself openly, and I don't keep diaries either, so I'm not sure how my stalker knows things he shouldn't about me or why I'm being continuously reminded of that time in my life. Not even my husband knew me this well.

I should throw the cake out, but I doubt the baker would poison me. He may deliver a note, but adding poison to a cake is unlikely.

I grab a fork and dig in. It is my birthday, after all. Again, something else my stalker knows that no one else does. Not once have I celebrated this day. I'm not even sure my father knew it, and my mother was too busy trying to protect us to know Monday from Wednesday.

After just one bite, my mouth waters. A hum leaves my lips, tasting the dense, thick frosting, sweet compared with the spices in the pumpkin mix. It's been too long since I've had a dessert like this. My stomach flutters with the indulgence. I take two more and start up the stairs, locking my door behind me. It's not the one I took the doctor to. I don't let anyone in this one, which is why I'm not sure how my stalker found me in it.

I toss the cake to the side and don't bother settling under the covers before lowering my hand between my legs. Fuck it. I'll give myself today to give in to the urges that have plagued me since seeing the masked man. His incessant need to shower me with gifts isn't going to impress me, but today… the throbbing between my legs was almost enough to get me off in that dress shop.

I may not use his money, but I'll use the memory of him. My skin comes alive just thinking about him showing himself after two years of not knowing who he is; if he was a man or woman, short or tall, old or young.

The lights are out, but I swear I feel him. The lack of sight heightens every other sense, letting me feel that raw darkness he's cloaked with. He wears a mask, but he doesn't hide who he is like everyone else, like me.

He laughs without shame, kills without mercy. He knows what he wants and he takes it. I'm jealous.

I close my eyes, imagining the black mask hovering over me, envisioning the intense gaze watching me like he wanted to in the dress shop. Again, my other senses grow increasingly sensitive to the coldness of my fingers sliding between my folds, the scent of the pumpkin and vanilla on the nightstand, and the sound of my hitching breath. Thinking of the masked stranger watching me from the corner has me already slick with need.

CRUEL KINGDOMS

"Did you save me a piece, little bird?"

My heart stops, but my hand doesn't. He isn't here, he can't be. I locked the door.

The bed sinks next to me; my hands are pulled above my head and secured within seconds. I jerk, but the rope tightens to the bedpost, biting into my wrists.

His body presses against mine as his mask grazes my cheek. I should, but I don't scream. The girls would wake, and I don't want them to see me or put them in his sights, though if he's watched me long enough, he knows all about them.

I'm hyper-aware that I'm only in my night slip, and while he's been in my mouth and has seen me naked twice today, for some reason, him straddling me on my bed is more intimate—more dangerous—and it's not because my hands are restrained.

"I came to give you a gift you can't return, but it looks like you started without me." His head angles toward the cake, dragging his gaze back between my legs where I'm on full display.

The room grows silent with only my rapid breathing exposing how fast my heart is pounding. I should have lit a candle so I could see better.

"What do you want? Really?" My question brings him back to me. His head angles to the other side curiously. When his fingers trace the emerald around my neck, I dig my head into the pillow, trying to get away from his touch. "Don't take it!"

I'm ready to beg him to let go, ready to do anything he asks of me if only he leaves the necklace alone, but I don't have to. Delicately, he places it in the center of my chest, leaning back in with his mask a breath away from me. I'm too focused on the patterns carved into it to realize he lifted the bottom until his mouth is on mine.

SINISTER DESIRE

His lips are soft. Mine open as his tongue pushes against mine for a better taste—vanilla.

"Want?" He lets out a sinister laugh that makes my stomach coil. "That insinuates I won't get it."

He must have had a sedative on his tongue or blessed with a one laced within his voice, like the devil himself would to lure us damned, because my head is growing as heavy as my body with every inch he slowly crawls down me.

His tongue drags around my nipple through the faux silk, his mouth wrapping around the taut bud. When he pulls it into his mouth and sucks, I swear I see stars.

His knees kick my legs apart as he settles himself between them, lying on top of me like I'm his favorite set of sheets.

My head is hazy at the reality before me. I have a voice, and yet, I can't find it. It's locked away with my sanity, digging itself deeper with every soft tug of his lips. My body is even more useless when he lifts himself up and pulls his shirt over his head.

If the mask wasn't my kink, his body is. It's dark, but I can make out the hard edges of his frame. My stomach quivers at the sight. The way this man is built should be illegal, he's too hard, too strong, too destructive. I don't know why I thought it was a good idea to challenge him.

He lowers himself back over me, and I'm suddenly aware that he could easily crush me. The authority and demand his voice holds is nothing compared to the control his body possesses. Everything he does is unhurried, taking his time to draw out every butterfly that's ever lived in my body, sending them into a chaotic rage in the pit of my stomach.

He moves to the other bud that's begging for attention, pulling the slip down to remove the barrier between him and what he's after, taking my nipple between his lips and tugging. At the nip of his teeth, I let out a heated whimper.

The mask shifts, letting me see the tiniest sliver of his plush bottom lip. He could be the most hideous man, but those dark eyes and that lip paint a very different picture in my head.

"You don't put up much of a fight when you're aroused."

"I am not—" his fingers trace between my legs, feeling my body's betrayal. "Is that what you want then? For me to fight?"

His amusement rattles against me as he lowers himself down my torso, his tongue teasing along my thighs. "Your fight is cute, but what I *want* is for you to relax and enjoy this gift before I make good on my earlier promise."

I don't know what promise he's talking about, but I toss his words to the wind when I realize what he's about to do. Richard had been too quick to get off to care about this and the men I meet in town pay to be selfish. I've only ever had one person between my legs like this, and it's bringing up a grief that I rather not remember right now.

"You don't have to do that." My breath is too needy for the fear I feel. He could kill me and my girls within minutes, and all I can think about is how much I hope he doesn't listen to the stupid words that just came out of my mouth.

His fingers tickle my skin as he slides the slip higher up my stomach, reaching until he finds the neckline of the slip and pulls it beneath my heavy breasts. His fingers continue the work where his mouth started. With his mask still up, he darts his tongue out and licks up my center, unrushed, both teasing and savoring. All previous thoughts are gone as my legs shake from the earlier build.

SINISTER DESIRE

One hand abandons my nipples to hold the inside of my thigh, keeping me still. I don't know what it is about that damn mask, but I'm on the edge within seconds.

He pulls his head back just enough that I still can't see his face. "Do you want me to stop?"

I should stop him, but my knee bends and my foot is pushing his head back where he belongs. He chuckles, knowing he won. I want to be angry that I let him, but I can't when he pulls at my nipple, twisting it between his fingers as his tongue continues circling that spot between my legs.

"Oh, I..." my hands wrap around the rope securing my wrists. My eyes threaten to close, but I don't want to look away. It feels like my entire body is going to explode into one of the black stars that start to fill my vision.

"My... I..." I don't even know why I'm trying to talk or what I'm trying to say.

It's the briefest sight of his tongue that's my undoing. The current that flows through me lights my entire body to life and sends my hips rocking against him.

I beg him to stop when everything grows too sensitive to the point of pain, but he continues feasting on me, widening my legs to fill me with his fingers one at a time. Every deliberate pump builds me right back up, dragging me closer to oblivion. With how heated my flesh is, it might be toward Hell—a delicious section where a demon like this man is made to torment me with too much pleasure.

I don't know when I start to lose consciousness, but I know it's after the third time he has me coming on his tongue and fingers. I'm so out of it that when he releases my hands, I don't have the energy to fight him off. I don't want to. He's put me in a state of frenzied sedation where my body buzzes with a need for both more and sleep.

I knock the mask away, but I can't see him in the dark, only his forehead and a mess of raven-black hair. Another piece to the stranger's puzzle.

"You're a fucking sin." His teeth graze my inner thigh, sucking the skin into his mouth. "You went to that fountain after I told you not to." He moves to the other thigh, repeating the same bite-and-suck combination, my flesh growing more sensitive with every one.

My head lulls to the side, too tired and dazed to lift my head or think of anything outside of listening to his voice.

"You forced my hand, and now I have to ensure that everyone knows you're off limits. That you're mine."

He said it before, *want* isn't in his vocabulary because he gets things he desires, and for whatever reason, he has his desires set on me. I'm not sure if I say it out loud, but I tell myself, "You can't have me," before utter exhaustion finally starts to take over.

"This is going to hurt, little bird."

I roll over, pinching my eyes tighter when the sun hits my face. I groan, groggier than I ever have been before. I'm never up after the sun.

With that thought, I dart awake, tossing the covers off me and jump out of bed. I stop when I notice the dark red marks plastered all over my body. My thighs, my chest. I lift my slip and see them up my stomach and my breasts. I rush to the washroom and find them up my neck.

SINISTER DESIRE

I'm a complete mess. My skin and cheeks are flush and pale at the same time, and my hair is a nest of brown tangles. My upper back is hot and sore.

I start to turn but notice the dried frosting on my chest reads one word, *mine*.

Flashes of last night rush to my foggy head. He was here. The cake box next to my bed is now empty, and flashes of him feeding it to me come to my mind.

As if my body remembers everything, my skin grows sensitive, feeling his tongue, hands, and tantalizing mouth over every inch of me.

After a long, steaming shower, I promise myself it was only one time. It was my birthday, and I indulged, just this once. I'll start sleeping with a knife under my pillow and ensure all windows and doors are locked through the day and night.

He's a murderer, I repeat over and over.

Naturally I lift my hand to wipe the mirror but stop when I see his note. Written with red lipstick on the foggy mirror, reads:

Tag, you're it.
You have until dawn to find me or it's my turn.
*-**Your** faithful follower*

CRUEL KINGDOMS

Faithful Follower

Sin. That's what she is and that's what she tastes like. Like something that should be locked away and given to those who are dying in small doses to bring them back to life.

I'm not humming hymns, but I sure as shit will only be speaking tongues on my knees for her.

Too much of her would kill any man. Maybe that's why they're all dead. I'm not like them, or any other man for that matter. I kill them. It's what I was trained to do—*born* to do. Specifically, men like the doctor.

Hate isn't a strong enough word for how much I loathe men or women who use their status and power to take advantage of or intimidate others. It doesn't matter if it's to impress a lover with their money or, like the doctor, fuck in exchange for something that should be free. It's disgusting and weak. Something only a coward twat would do because they're too lazy to put in the work.

Things worth having are worth a few bruises, and the thing I have my eye on is worth risking it all.

My little bird never knew who I really was when we first met, and she won't know who I am now until I know she can handle me. Until she sees me at my worst, at my core, and accepts it.

"She's going to hate you," Duke mutters as his right hook just misses my face.

SINISTER DESIRE

I shrug, sweat pouring down my forehead and chest, keeping my hands high as we circle between the trees. Our sweat and blood have hydrated more of these woods than rainwater over the years.

"She'll only *think* she hates me until she realizes I did it for her protection."

Duke scoffs, taking another swing that lands against my chin, followed by a blow to my gut. My breath is knocked from me but I'm trained well enough to counter while down. Using my bent-over position, I wrap my arms around his waist and tackle him to the dirt.

Duke isn't a small man, practically the same shape and build as me except for the brown hair and collection of scars and tattoos that hold too many stories, most I was a part of. My knuckles land on his most recent scar, a matching one to mine near my ribs where a corrupt priest got the best of us. We were so far undercover that by the time we found the boy he locked in his attic to lure the woman he was obsessed with, we could preach verses verbatim out of that damn bible.

He struggles under me, but he's placating me, letting me release all of the tension and excess energy that's been building before I do something stupid. "Keep telling yourself that, Death. We both know you marked her for your own obsessive need to possess and claim her."

Death. That was the name given to me when I was recruited into The Trove. Duke isn't his real name, just as Death isn't mine. We're all prominent in some way and willing to use our connections and specialties to aid in silently ridding the world of the sick corruption that plagues it. Duke has this ability to get anyone to like and trust him in ways I never could, which is why he's usually the one who's sent in first to gather our target's trust before I'm sent to finish our task.

I apply my full body weight down onto his shoulders to keep him down so he listens to me clearly. "You get to criticize me when your own problems have been dealt with. What do you call her? A thorn in your side?"

I'm on my back within seconds, with Duke's death glare drilling into me as hard as his fists strikes my ribs again and again. "There's the thorn in your side, asshole."

He lifts himself off me with an offered hand that I don't take. My body is bruised, sore, and bloody. The soft wind in the air feels too good on my steaming skin.

All that work to clear my mind for a few hours and it's gone in a catch of a breath. I can't get my little bird's clean scent or sweet taste away. The image of her writhing beneath me, because of me, is forever branded in my mind. It's all I see when I close them.

I couldn't stop after just one taste. It nearly killed me to pull away to ask if she wanted me to. Part of me was fucking with her the same way she teased me when she licked me base to tip, pulling away to let her saliva string between us. The minx tests my control in ways I need to study so I can master it before I lose it completely.

Questioning if she wanted me to stop was rhetorical and timed just right so she would beg me to continue—a choice, and she not only chose correctly, but she took me by surprise when she forced me back into her. My black heart filled with pride seeing her want something and take it, and with a fucking smile. I didn't want it to go away, so I kept going and going. I needed her tired anyway.

I needed today, this combat with Duke, to tire me out before I head to her. This game I'm playing has a purpose, one that started two years ago when I sent my first letter. If there's anything I've learned during the years that I thought I'd lost her, it's that I'm a patient man, but even my patience has its limits.

SINISTER DESIRE

"You boys really are brutes." Our heads turn to find the third in our group. The one who gathers intel before Duke infiltrates, and I'm sent to finish. Her disguise is still heavy in place when she says the last thing I want to hear. "We have a problem."

Chapter Seven

The hours pass slower than they should. In the distance I hear the clock tower striking every hour, something I usually don't pay any mind to or notice.

I had one appointment today, but with the murders and the markings all over my body, I decided to cancel. Not out of fear for myself but for others. What if my faithful follower shows up and kills the guard who's supposed to meet with me? Or what if someone in town notices all the bruised hickeys?

Instead, I send the twins to town to meet with Lucy and send Ember to buy something for herself as a belated birthday gift, giving them all coin I *earned* from both the dollmaker and my faithful follower.

With the girls away, I find myself passing the empty chicken coop, the empty horse stalls, and walking down the rocky path that was once lush with greenery and blooming flowers. The once perfectly placed stone steps are now a dreadful sight, cracked and covered with dirt. The flowerbeds are now full of weeds that grow tall and wild.

I don't bother with the crumbling bench and instead, drop myself to the ground, rest my back against the pear tree, and sink my toes into the cold dirt. We all have strange comforts, and this is mine.

Seeing the markings on my body brought me back to being a child when my mother wore bruises like they were her favorite accessory. The ones I wear aren't painful, and they weren't caused by hatred, but the sight unlocked memories I had thought I buried in the darkest parts of my subconscious.

Back then, when my father's drunken fists were flying, I listened to my mother and ran. I would find a new garden and sink my feet into the cold soil to soothe my sore feet and wait. I couldn't bury myself to soothe the rest of my body after my mother died, but I still ran when he was done.

The markings on me aren't the same; I know that. The thing is hickeys and bruises are both made with an uncontrollable desire to leave a mark. And while I stand by my words—my stalker will *not* own me—why do I have my own sinister desire to mark him back?

My feet dig deeper into the dirt as I think about all the death in the air.

The harlots who have died, or *widowed whores* as whispers call us, didn't deserve it. Like everyone else, they were just trying to survive. Mallory told me about the others in passing and warnings, like when one girl almost got caught in the church because she forgot to check the confessional. I didn't know her, but she taught me that taking precautions was just as important as performing.

I never knew the other's names, only Mallory's. She was the madame who told us all who to meet, when, where, the price, and the kinks, all written on a simple bookmark in code.

It's her death that lies heavy on me now. Did she have a family? Did the dollmaker? Dr. Douglas had a wife who had her own affairs. Has she noticed him missing yet?

If I hadn't gone to that fountain, maybe they would all still be alive. Maybe if I hadn't run away that day, my mother wouldn't have died at my father's hands. She is why I have a soft spot for Ember. I know exactly what it's like to lose a mother so young. How that missing piece never gets filled again.

CRUEL KINGDOMS

Unfortunately for me, my father waited to die after he sold me to Richard at fifteen. I made my husband swear the twins would never have to see him, and that was the only promise he kept.

Little did I know, we were his secret family he hid away from his real wife and daughter, Ember and her mother. It wasn't until after I confronted him about a letter that I found his fists started swinging too.

I turned out just like my mother, in an abused marriage, doing whatever I could to protect my daughters. The only difference is I survived when she didn't.

I find myself in the same sanctuary I sought ten years ago after the first blow. I tried to leave, but Richard locked me in the attic for a week and sent the girls away for a month to prove that he could take them away from me anytime he wanted. I didn't try to leave again and thanked him often for not letting the girls see him as the wicked man he was.

The clock strike startles me back to the present.

Dawn. *He's it.*

I straighten my spine and grip the knife tighter in my palm. My senses heighten as my widened gaze dart to every corner of the ghastly garden. The feeling of being watched takes hold.

I wait, counting my breaths.

"Lady Audrey," a familiar voice calls my name.

"Gus?" I let out a breath. The groundskeeper turns his head in my direction. "What are you doing here? I thought you already came this month?"

SINISTER DESIRE

I can't afford any help, but Gus said he didn't feel right leaving us with nothing, so he stops by once a month to check in and fix things around the house. He comes in handy when something breaks or when the fireplace needs cleaning. Part of me feels bad, but he never asks for anything except a plate at dinner and a glass of wine.

"It's Ember's Birthday," he says, stomping through the weeds to meet me. The man is massive and takes them down with ease. I wouldn't put it past him to be able to push this tree over with his bare hands. "Well, yesterday. I stopped by, but no one answered. I just wanted to drop off a gift. I figured I'd poke around and see if there was anything I could do before I left."

His eyes fall to my neck, and then the knife cradled against my chest. My cheeks burn with embarrassment. I planned to be alone for hours and didn't bother covering up. "Oh… I was—"

He held his hand up to silence me. "It's none of my business. But I recommend you keep that knife close by with that serial killer on the loose."

My eyes turn into slits, trying to sound offended. "He targets harlots. Do I look like one to you?"

It's his turn to grow red. "That's not what I meant. I—" he huffs. I think it's the first time I've ever seen him agitated. "Jack is out of jail, and with Ember turning eighteen, I think you should know he'll likely stop by to try to collect her and her dowry. He's her only living male relative, and with you having to worry about your girls, he'll claim there's a conflict of interest with you finding her a suitor."

"He's not taking her." Every word leaves my mouth as its own personal sentence. I'm not handing her over to that gambling addict who would spend her dowry faster than he could count it. And that's saying a lot, considering there isn't one. When he finds out Richard emptied all three dowries the week before he died, he'll sell Ember to the fastest bidder for quick money just like my own father did to me.

Gus' face sours. "If you need me to come around more, just in case, I can. Each time he gets out, he's a little meaner. A little needier, too."

"Thank you for telling me, but I'm sure we'll be fine. I'll send him on his way like the last two times he tried."

He doesn't look convinced. "I'll stop by when I can anyway."

I'm grateful for the offer and start to nod, then remember the time. I glance around the garden again, but that feeling of being watched doesn't return. Two things strike me at the same time: either Gus is my stalker, or he's in line to be his next victim.

"Since you're here, do you want leftover cake?" I take his arm in mine and hurry back toward the house. "I think I have a few more bottles of wine we can open?"

Gus' smile nearly splits his face. I can't see him being the one who stabbed the dollmaker in the neck and then used my mouth like his right hand. He's always been one to wave and smile at everyone. His cheeky grin and smiley eyes put a smile on everyone's face. Thinking of this giant teddy bear murdering the doctor and then sneaking into my room to feed me cake and feast on me was impossible—okay, the second half of that thought I can imagine, but not the murder.

He's two glasses and two pieces of cake deep when his tongue loosens a bit. "Why…I'm sorry I shouldn't ask, but what happened?"

I follow where his eyes land back on my neck. If this were anyone but Gus, I would question if he were jealous, but the man never looked at me that way. Or at least, I never noticed it. If he had, well, he was handsome: my age, tall, and built like a tree. Black hair… in fact, the more I look at him, the more I'm convincing myself that he is my stalker.

SINISTER DESIRE

If he is, why send notes? And why start two years ago?

I clear my throat with an idea to test this theory. "This wine is going straight to my head." I giggle and toss my robe to the side, leaving me in a simple dress that leaves little to the imagination. His eyes widen when he sees more markings down my chest.

"Audrey…" his voice is filled with concern.

"It was an accident."

His jaw tightens. "I've seen your *accidents* before, and they were never like this." My head spins at his admission. He knew what Richard did to me? "You were never good at hiding bruises. Who did this to you?"

"A persistent man."

His hand catches mine on the table. It's the longest minute of my life, looking into his eyes and lips, silently suggesting that I want a taste until he gently pulls me forward. I'm lifted from my chair and settle on him. He's so tall that even in his lap, I'm not looking down on him. I can feel him hard beneath me, but he doesn't bring any attention to it. Instead, he leans in and softly nuzzles my neck, placing the softest kiss on the mark there.

My blood heats. All I can focus on is where his hand slowly lifts my dress higher up my legs with the slightest hesitation.

I don't need to ask the next thing to confirm what I already know, but I do anyway. I need to hear him say it to rid the thought from my mind. "Where's the mask?"

He doesn't stop kissing my neck as he asks, "What mask?"

Chapter Eight

I was ready to stop Gus, but I didn't have to once the girls came home within a second after I confirmed Gus wasn't my faithful follower. I knew when he didn't give that dark chuckle or grip me possessively. My stalker wouldn't hesitate to lift my dress or suck on my neck. Gus was too gentle, and where my stalker had been gentle to pleasure me that night, there was a forced control to him. Where his kisses were soft, his hands were hard, and if his hands softened, then his mouth grew more needy. And the eyes... My stalker has an intensity that is unmistakable, even behind that distressed mask.

It's been five days since I've heard from him. He didn't come at dawn or leave any notes or gifts. I don't care about the gifts, I won't use them, but he came into my life like a damn demon ready to raise Hell, only to turn into a ghost who's silently haunting me. The same way he's haunted me for two years, one of them in complete silence.

I went to the rest of the appointments that were listed on the bookmark, and maybe it was a bit homicidal knowing he could show up to kill the men at any second, but I waited for him with bated breath anyway. I kept my eyes open and put on the best shows of my life in case he was watching.

This is how I felt a year ago when his notes stopped, anxious with the slightest bit of fear and agitation—betrayed. For a while, I thought Richard was my stalker because they ended after his death, but that never made sense, considering the contents of them.

SINISTER DESIRE

This time is different. I'm tired of looking over my shoulder, waiting for him. With every passing second he doesn't show, I should be relieved, but I can't stop the prickle in my skin knowing he lied to me, *again*. He didn't give me a time when he was going to find me, but it's implied not to be a week away.

I'm re-lacing my dress in the empty church, ready to walk out of my last appointment, when it hits me: I no longer have a madam who will supply the appointments. I ask the guard how he makes the arrangements, but he gives me a questioning look, pushes me back to my knees, and tells me to mind my business and keep my mouth shut by doing its job.

I'm not great with change. Routine is the key to life. And what really pushes me over my limits? This guard thinking he can get off again on *my* time.

With one hand on the back of my head, he makes a point to put the other on the hilt of his sword. "You don't question royal guards, harlot. Unless you are asking to suck my cock again. Do you understand?" He starts to unsheathe his sword to prove his point.

My stalker's voice plays in the back of my mind. He's using his position to get what he wants. He's taking advantage, making me weak.

I can't continue to be that girl.

With as much force as I can muster, I push off his thighs. His sword is at my throat within a second. He doesn't wait or use his words to threaten me this time. The tip of his blade reaches the neckline of my dress, slicing through the corset.

I take one breath when I confirm he didn't cut my skin. I don't get a chance to look back up before he drops his weapon to rip the rest of the silk away with his bare hands before turning me over.

CRUEL KINGDOMS

I've never felt weaker than I do as he shoves me into a pew and yanks the back of my dress down. My head remains bowed against the wood as I wait for the inevitable, knowing I'm no match for a man of his stature or his sword, but the assault doesn't come. All I can think is how I should have brought the knife I've taken to sleeping with under my pillow. Little good it's doing there.

I hear the shuffling of clothes, feel something cover my back, and hear him grumbling curses before the front door slams shut.

I'm not sure why the guard ran off, but I'm grateful he left me his cloak. My dress was unsalvageable, and I would have either had to walk home naked or use the Bibles to cover myself up.

The sun is setting by the time I muster the courage to rush out of the church as fast as I can, my head low and hidden under the hood. My focus is on my feet when someone hits my shoulder, knocking us both to the ground. My hands are in a flurry, gathering the dark blue fabric to ensure my naked body is still covered.

The brunette woman rubbing her collarbone almost mimics my movement but for her dress. It's the book she hurries to grab, the familiar bookmark sticking out of the top that catches my eye. Her eyes don't meet mine as she offers a quick apology, jumps to her feet, and rushes into the church I just left.

People pass in a hurry, going about their afternoon routines as I climb to my feet and brush away any debris. That's when I feel eyes on me. It doesn't matter that I shove the hood back over my head; someone is following me; I can feel it. I turn back to my path, finding only one peculiar person: the old woman with white hair and even whiter eyes is leaning against a building, shuffling a deck of cards with her eyes on me. Just like before, she offers a small wave.

SINISTER DESIRE

By the time I'm back home, I can't relax into a regular routine or so much as run upstairs to shower. I snag a drying dress from the outside line, change behind one of the trees, and head inside to find the table set with bowls and Ember singing in the kitchen with a damn window open, stirring a pot in a rhythm that matches the song.

"What are you making?" I ask, not hiding my surprise. Ember never steps foot in the kitchen unless it's to make a mess; leaving bowls on the counter and mixing odd ingredients, I'm sure, is only to make the kitchen stink.

"I'm making soup. It was my father's favorite. Since we didn't honor him earlier this week, I figured we could tonight."

"That's thoughtful of you," I praise, commending any effort she makes. I'm not sure where this idea comes from when my late husband never ate soup, favoring a baked potato overloaded with bacon. His poor diet never messed with his strong form, though. The man ran every morning and night around the property to keep in shape while limiting my food to ensure I kept mine.

"You act like he was just your father," Dee sneers as Ally nods in agreement. Neither of them hides their visible suspicions as Ember pours them each a ladle of soup that looks and smells of too many seasonings: peppers, paprika, garlic, onion, and something spicy. There's corn, carrots, and chunks of potatoes simmering in the steaming murky broth. I ignore their argument as I spoon around the broth to see floating meat that doesn't look appetizing at all.

When I look back up, Ember's smirking at me like she knows something she shouldn't. "What are you waiting for?" she asks, taking a spoonful into her mouth.

The girls exhale, realizing they aren't about to be poisoned. The same shiver of relief passes through me as I take my first bite. The spoon hasn't left my mouth before the back of my throat clenches to keep from spitting it back up. Quickly I grab a napkin and spit my mouthful into it. "What is this you made?" I ask.

I cough to grab my girl's attention, waiting until Ember looks away to shake my head. They know how to discard unwanted food properly, but I need them to know it's okay. Ember would have caught on if she bothered attending the etiquette classes I paid for.

"Corn, Carrots, lots of seasonings I found in the cabinets, and meat." Ember took another bite.

"What kind of meat, darling?"

Ember smiles, taking another bite. "Rats."

"Rats?!" Ally yells, jumping up from the table. "You fed us rats?"

"What's wrong with that?" Ember shrugs. "I thought we needed to save money. I cut them up myself. I didn't even need a butcher."

Dee squirms and grunts with disgust. "You psychopath!" Both girls run upstairs. The faucets echo from their bathroom, along with their gags.

"Ember." I lean back in my seat, seemingly unbothered when inside I'm fuming.

"Yes, Lady Audrey?" She takes another bite.

"Quit eating. You'll get sick."

"It's not that bad." She's not done chewing before forcing in another bite to prove a point.

"They have diseases."

SINISTER DESIRE

"You probably do, too, after what you do all day," she says, swaying her head from side to side as if a song were playing.

The control I'm maintaining not to react should really be commendable. "What does that mean?"

"I know what you do all day is all. You can catch diseases that way too."

I swear I must not have heard her correctly. There is no possible way she knows what I do. I never bring anyone home. I lock the lists away. She has to be testing the waters, baiting me into an argument.

An icy calmness comes over me. "Why do you insist on playing these games? Fighting with the girls? Arguing and challenging me at every turn?"

"Because I don't like you." The words aren't a surprise, but the fact that she voiced them so casually is. This has always been a game, both of us knowing we don't favor the other, but trying to appear as if we do. Our only unspoken agreement is that we don't say it out loud, ever. "And I know you don't like me, just like I know you're not taking me to the ball because you only have two dresses."

"That's all I can afford right now. *You* will be going. You have my word." If one of my own daughters has to sit out, I'll send this girl just for the chance to get her married off sooner. The issue is she doesn't have any manners and doesn't care to learn any, which isn't likely to attract any potential suitors, specifically one who will be able to care for her like she needs. She might be eighteen, but she still acts like a child.

"And you don't go back on your word? Right. So, you must have bought the tickets that cost a fortune, too?" She giggles to herself before slurping on the soup. "I can only imagine the things you had to do for those."

My hand's moving before I can even think about what I'm doing. The soup flies through the air. The bowl clanks as it hits the opposite wall and falls to the floor, shattering.

CRUEL KINGDOMS

Ember jumps back in surprise, but I storm toward her and grip her chin so she can't look away from me. "I. Said. Stop. Eating."

Her blue eyes flash with terror, and it's that moment that I realize the power my father felt. The power they all feel.

A knock at the backdoor startles us both. My hand tightens slightly before letting her chin go with a soft shove. I'm not violent, and I refuse to let myself go any further than that. At least, I hope so. There is a rush buzzing through me that I don't find appealing in the slightest. Like when you're caught in the rain, your hair and makeup are a mess, your clothes are sticky, you're starting to shiver, and all you want to do is be warm again.

I open the door.

I expected the man before me to show up one day. His red leather jacket stinks of weed and whisky as his eyes rake up my body with a sly lick of his lips. He holds a note out between his fingers. My heart shoots to my throat. "This was on your porch."

I reach to grab it, but he holds it higher so I can't. "What's it worth to you?"

I roll my eyes and jump to snatch it before he can rip it. He takes my distraction as opportunity to shove my shoulder with his to let himself in. Water from the pouring rain puddles all over the tile flooring.

"Ember, my favorite niece!" He ruffles her hair with his tattooed fist. His boots are heavy as he makes his way to my seat, plopping himself into it and taking a bite of the foul soup. "Audrey, we should talk about my dear niece here. You have a few minutes, don't you?"

My eyes don't leave his and I don't bother to hide my glare.

"Ember, can you give us a minute?"

She crosses her arms and shakes her head. "I'm eighteen. I should be a part of this conversation."

"Fine." I do the same as I focus on her insolent uncle. "What is it you want to discuss, Jack?"

His smile would be handsome if he weren't a complete sleaze. It's so similar to Ember's—kind, to any stranger who doesn't know them. His slender form in the oversized jacket only accentuates his rugged appearance.

"I want Ember, and I want her dowry. You have two girls of your own to worry about. Let me take my niece off your hands." His straight-to-the-point tone is giving me pause. He's usually one to ramble with ideas, not present them like a lawyer.

"No," I say without hesitation.

Ember scoffs. "But he's right. You haven't secured me anything. There are no suitors. No one is knocking on our door for me."

"No one is knocking on the door because your father pulled all the money from your dowry."

"What?!" Jack's hand slams against the table, rattling the remaining dishes. "Liar!" The cool he came in with is gone, replaced with the Jack I remember. The chaotic one who flies off the handle when opposed.

"Not even my own girls have a dowry. He cleared all of them the week before he died. You can ask the bank yourself."

"I will." He slowly stands, hooding his eyes to intimidate me. He knows nothing about the men I've dealt with my entire life. It's almost cute the way he thinks he can make me shudder with fear at the mere sight of him. "And I will be back to collect."

"Uncle Jack, take me with you!" Ember follows him to the door.

"Not now, Emmy, but soon," he promises, slamming the door behind him.

She spins to face me, her blonde locks whipping across her face. "Why can't you just let me go with him?" she screams like a child who is being denied a second dessert.

"You heard what he said when you asked to go. He said not now. He doesn't want you. He wants your money."

Her lips tremble. That might have been too direct. "Why are you so cold? You're just a bitter, cruel, and jealous woman. You don't want me to succeed, do you?"

"We can talk about this in the morning." A headache's forming in the front of my head, and I'm not entirely sure it isn't because of the rats.

"You forget, it's Friday tomorrow, which means you'll be up and out of the door before any of us are even awake." She turns on her heel and stomps up the stairs, where the gagging is still echoing down the hallways.

I wait ten minutes to ensure no one is around before opening the note.

I'll give you a second chance.
Find me in the garden tonight, or I'm coming back inside, and this time, I don't care if the girls hear.

SINISTER DESIRE

Chapter Nine

I must be insane to be sneaking out of my house to meet a stalker—murderer—in the middle of the night in the pouring rain. I'm not two steps out of the door, and my hair is soaked. I don't know why I grab a robe when all it does is make my shoulders heavy. In a way it feels like my armor.

Every step I take makes me more aware that I can't see clearly or hear anything out of the ordinary with how hard the rain falls, pattering against the walkway with the wind rustling the twiggy branches and fallen leaves around me.

When the hair on the back of my neck stands, I know he's here. Somewhere.

The sliver of the moon provides the slightest glimmer of light, revealing frightful shadows that expose how haunted this property is. The barren trees sway with the gust of wind as debris and leaves tumble through the air.

Naturally, my feet take me down the path to my usual spot. I don't expect he'll be sitting there, waiting for me, to tell me that I've won and the game is over.

It dawns on me now, walking toward what could very well be my death, that I've never even asked him who he is. I've been so enamored

CRUEL KINGDOMS

with the mask and in shock over the murders that it never occurred to me to simply ask.

A note hangs from the pear tree.

Too late, I'm it.
Run, little bird.

The weeds rustle too harshly for it to be the wind.

I turn and find the black mask rising from where he's crouched in the tall weeds. He looks like the image of death, waking up from his slumber with his eyes set on me. For a moment, I'm stuck, shamelessly fixated on the sight of his broad naked chest, of him walking toward me with only carnal promise. Dark, violent bruises paint the side of his ribs.

I bite my lip and shake my head. *Fuck him.* He doesn't get to call on me when he wants me. Make me wait days for him and then show up and demand this game.

I turn and run. His footsteps pick up behind me as I sprint. Never have I had a bigger motivation to keep running than to prove to this man that I'm not his.

The water hitting my face doesn't help, but at least I know these grounds. I don't need to see clearly to maze through the familiar layout.

I stumble when my robe catches on something. It sends my blood pumping faster. I shed it quickly, pulling my arms from the sleeves, spotting him not far behind me, and take off again.

There's one place he wouldn't look for me. I turn to the right, passing a fallen statue where peonies used to grow. I turn right again, left then right, spotting the pear tree once again. I look behind me with a smile I can't hide when I don't see him, just eerie branches. I've lost him.

SINISTER DESIRE

I take a breath to regulate my body, to calm down the adrenaline coursing through me as I lower myself into the small fountain and place one of the tumbled weeds over myself. The thorns poke, but I cover my mouth to keep from making any sudden noises.

My heart pumps through my skin with the heated thrill of being chased. The terror of being caught. It's not long before I hear footsteps slowing, and that throbbing between my legs syncs up with him. *Traitor.*

I peek my eyes open and see the hard muscles on his back, his head swiveling back and forth, searching for me.

"I know you're here, little bird."

His voice does something to me that I don't want to acknowledge right now. When he turns again, I see the knife glisten in his hand. I recognize it as the one I hid under my pillow.

Why didn't I grab one before coming out here?

I suck in a breath. He turns.

I don't get a chance to flinch before his hands are on me, dragging me out of the fountain. I struggle, but he's too strong.

The ground is so wet and slick, I get lucky when he slips, loosening his hold. I take the chance to run again. I make my way around the fountain and behind the pear tree when I'm tackled to the ground, my head landing hard on his hand.

I'm flipped onto my stomach, his weight heavy on my back. My dress is caked in blood, soaked, and torn so thoroughly that I feel his fingers run up my bare spine rather than through fabric. Tearing cloth reaches my ears, my skin prickling, back shivering, exposed in the cold night breeze.

CRUEL KINGDOMS

The knife stabs the dirt near my head—*my* knife. "What were you going to do with this?"

I don't answer. I have to physically bite my lip not to because all I want is to yell at him right now.

"I'm waiting, little bird."

I try to push my weight to my knees, but he's straddling my waist with his legs on either side of me, keeping me pinned in place.

I let out a frustrated huff.

"I have all night."

"Oh, do you? You mean you're not too busy?" I shove my head into the dirt, hoping it'll bury me deep before he can see my blush.

His throaty laugh sounds like a twisted song with the rain pattering as his choir. "Did you miss me that much?"

"No."

"Strange," he leans into my ear and lowers his voice to a sultry whisper. "I didn't take you for a liar." He pauses, lifting my hair out of my face to see me better. "I have another question, and I hope you answer honestly this time."

My heart stills, filled with suspense.

"Why do you have a royal cloak in your room?" It's my turn to laugh, but mine isn't as pretty. It's mocking because, for once, he doesn't know something about me. "Have you been seeing your clients?"

His question puts a sour taste in my mouth. I wouldn't have been so performative if I knew he wasn't watching.

SINISTER DESIRE

He pushes himself against my leg, letting me feel how ready he is. "Is this the only way you'll use the gifts I give you?"

A sharp sting hits my ass when I refuse to answer. I cry out. His hand is on my mouth to muffle the noise. *Thank you* is on the tip of my tongue for remembering the girls. I would die if they walked out to the scene.

He repeats the question, and I feel him lower his pants. "I don't want your charity," I belt out. This isn't like the guard who tried to attack me, and I can't explain why other than the way the man behind me makes me feel—infuriated and delirious with a need to yell at him before hoping he stops me with his throaty chuckle and soft lips.

"And I don't want yours. If it's a transaction you want, I'll give it to you." He leans into my ear, tickling my neck with his whisper, "Just say the words. Tell me you'll use my gifts if I fuck you."

I hold my tongue. He reaches beneath me and pulls down the top of my dress, cupping my breasts before teasing my nipples between his fingers. I hate that my body responds to him so well. Hate that he's making me squirm and it's somehow making me more turned on.

He's lined up, waiting for me, teasing me with the weapon I know the taste of. I nod with real need as my center trembles with it, needing more. "I'll use your money if you fuck me."

The last word isn't out before he starts to slide into me. Slowly, he retreats, giving me a few shallow thrusts before driving into me completely. It's a good thing his hand is over my mouth, smothering the moan that comes out from my very soul. I've been with a lot of men but this… I catch sight of his mask from the corner of my eye. This is different. He doesn't fuck me fast or try to be slow and sensual. He fills me with purpose.

His fingers continue to tease my nipple as he retreats and moves back in. Even when he's all the way in, it feels like he's trying to go deeper, hitting spots I didn't know existed. It's like he's trying to climb into my damn body.

I'm not entirely sure my previous thought about him being the image of death is wrong because it sure as hell feels like he's here for the sole purpose of making sure he doesn't leave my soul behind.

The mask lands between my face and the knife. With his hand around my neck, he pulls my head back and his lips crash against mine before I get a chance to peek at his face. His tongue pushes past my lips, claiming my mouth like he deserves it. There is no want here; it's all possession.

He ups his pace, and his harshness makes me want to run away just so he can catch me again. *Maybe...*

I reach for the knife. He grips my hands before I even touch it, bringing them above my head. "You want to keep playing?" His breath tickles my ear.

He grabs his mask and is off of me within seconds, leaving me empty and cold without his body to block mine from the pouring rain. I turn to face him. With the mask securely back on, he nods toward the knife in my hand and then toward the rest of the garden. "Run, little bird."

My eyes land on his bruised ribs, but I can't think about what could have caused such damage when he takes a step forward. I turn and sprint before he can see the smile that lifts on my face. I forgot how exhilarating it is to be chased, to hide...the way the rest of the world and its problems fade away when your sole focus is on survival—on winning.

I make it down the path and turn right when I'm tackled again, his hands pinning my shoulder down as he hovers over me. "I win again," he boasts.

SINISTER DESIRE

With the knife still in my hand, I don't wait for him to rip my dress to cut it away myself. My body is too alert, too deprived from the minute he left me to wait any longer.

He watches, his eyes following the knife slice through the torn and muddied fabric. My goose-prickled skin waits as an offering before him. My nipples hardened in the cold breeze—under his gaze.

The knife drops away pathetically when his mouth wraps around them, heating every piece of me.

He shifts between my legs and I don't get a breath before he's back inside me. I cover my mouth, moaning freely beneath it while staring into that black mask above me. He grips my knees, pushing them out farther to drive in deeper. I only last two more thrusts before I'm tightening around him with his growing pace.

There's something about this man gripping the dirt next to my head with one hand and my ass with the other that lengthens my ecstasy. I'm still throbbing as his hips move deeper, slower, finishing with groans that ring in my ears. "Fuck, little bird."

Neither of us moves, and it strikes me that he's *still* inside of me.

I use contraceptives, so I don't panic, but a sliver of fury fights its way through. "You can't just do that inside of me!" I slap his shoulder with real strength behind it.

"Why not?" He purrs against my neck. "You'll have all my children anyway."

The image of my pregnant belly flashes before me. I can see the scene play out in my head: me making dinner for this man who is covered in blood that isn't his, a baby playing with a collection of knives as toys. He can't be serious.

CRUEL KINGDOMS

I push him off me and try to stand. I'm sore, but I force myself to walk away. Walk isn't the right term. My feet are dragging through the dirt, and I'm ready to take a break after a few fumbling steps send prickles of sweet pain through my core. "Are you running from me, bird?"

"You won your game." I lift my hand and don't look back as I wave.

Heavy footsteps rush behind me.

SINISTER DESIRE

Faithful Follower

The sight of my little bird walking away from me again, this time by her own free will, hurt worse than the damn bruises covering half of my body. This is why I need my sparing with Duke before I see her. The energy buzzing through me is too much to control.

By the time the night's over, she won't be walking back to that house.

My arms wrap around her waist. I'm taking her to the ground and back inside of her before I can think about what I'm doing.

That's a lie. I'm completely aware of my sole focus right now; that's the problem.

She groans under me but not in pain. Her teeth catch her lip as her hands grasp at the dirt for anything to hold onto. I wrap my hand under her chin and pull her up to look at me, creating an arch in her back that only drives me in deeper.

"I'm sorry. Let me try that again the way you want this time. Your back? Stomach? Down that pretty throat again?" Her eyes flutter, and I know she's remembering the dress shop. She can't see it, but it puts a smile on my face, knowing she's already filled with memories of me, *more* memories of me.

Gripping her neck so she can still breathe, I pull her back even more so she's on her hands and knees and give her ass a soft slap for ignoring me. "We have an agreement. I fuck you, you spend my money and use my gifts. I have a lot to give, and the night is still young."

She looks up at me through rain-dripping lashes, her lips parted with awe. "Who are you?"

CRUEL KINGDOMS

She clenches around me, and my focus falls to where my body merges with hers. It's not the answer she wants, but it's no less true. "Yours."

Her mouth widens as she lets out a heavy breath. She might think I'm dangerous, I am, but she has no idea the danger she possesses when she looks at me like that. I pull out only to bring myself right back into her. The warmth alone makes me never want to leave, but it's her sharp moan that has me gripping her hip and making the effort to push myself in even deeper.

For the briefest second, we're back in time, until her brows crinkle, and the look of betrayal laces her voice as she says, "Then where were you?"

The ecstasy vanishes from my body. It's not her, but the flash of where I was that has me pulling out. I won't ever lie to her, but I can also see the hidden rage building inside the shaky glower she's throwing at me. This isn't about where I was but why I wasn't here.

Fuck. I knew leaving for five days was going to be a mistake.

She doesn't pull away when I spin her around and settle her so she's between my legs with my arms tight around her waist. Possessive or not, I don't want her trying to run away again.

"What happened?" No matter how hard I try, I can't shake the dominance from my voice when I question or give orders, not even with her.

The greens in her eyes darken with whatever rage is inside of her, and I'm ready for whatever she has.

A stream of manic thoughts is what I get, from Ember feeding them rats to some fucker called Jack showing up to intimidate her. Her cheeks crimson when she tells me how she met with her clients and performed as if I were watching, and then that rage returns as she mentions the guard I already know about, the one who tried to assault her.

I don't stop her or react, or at least I try not to. My knuckles are white from how hard I'm fisting my hands, and my shoulders are tensing with a need to spar or fuck my wrath out.

"I just… ever since you came back into my life, everything has been falling apart. Being a harlot has always been easy, but you come in and make me realize that I've been a fool this entire time. That I'm too passive and prideful. I…" she turns away, hot with embarrassment, "I don't need you to protect me, but I hate that you make me feel protected anyway."

Something warms in my chest. I want nothing more than to rip this mask off and kiss her, but she still isn't ready. She was always a caged bird; she's only now seeing that there's a door. That I broke the fucking hinges off that thing, so she'll never be locked away again.

I cusp the back of her neck and veer her head so she stops looking away. "I knew you were obsessed with me." I watch the anger disintegrate before my eyes as her lips tug and threaten to smile before she can't hold back the choked laugh that escapes her. "It sounds like you're finally ready to accept that you're mine. That I'm good for you."

This laugh isn't the mocking one she gave earlier when she thought I didn't know what she had done this week. I only asked to see if she'd tell me the truth.

I had eyes on her while Duke and I were away, reporting to me that she had been meeting with clients. Dove, my third, told me that she witnessed the guard leave the church white as snow and Audrey following after in only his cloak. If anyone knows what an assaulted woman looks like, it's Dove.

Duke and Dove are still working on tracking him down, along with the serial killer still at large. Needless to say, we've been busy.

CRUEL KINGDOMS

Audrey's laughs turn into giggles. Her hand on my chest lowers to the bruise still tender under her cold fingers. I don't take orders, but one soft shove and my body follows her silent command to lay back, taking me by surprise when she straddles my waist.

With one hand on my chest to steady herself, she reaches between us, fisting me with her palm to guide me back into her. I could help her, but I like watching her make the effort. Watching and listening to the shallow breaths she takes the lower she slides herself onto me until I'm fully sheathed inside her.

Her fingers trace along my bruises as she leans into my neck with a soft whisper, "How did you get this?"

Her tongue drags along my neck until she finds a spot she likes, presses her lips, and sucks.

My throat bobs with the guttural groan when she rocks her hips. The slow torture has my blood rushing straight to my head, seducing the sanity out of it. "Men who didn't want to die gave it their best efforts not to."

The problem Dove came in with five days ago was in a neighboring Kingdom. Normally, we wouldn't work so fast, but there was a possibility that it was connected to the harlot killings happening here. Turns out it had nothing to do with it. The harlot who went missing wasn't a harlot at all, but a princess who was almost sold overseas in an attempt to get rid of her by her younger sister. We found her in the freezer, where I was stuck for two days. When the men who purchased her showed, it was brutal. I was unconscious for another two days, nursed by Duke, who will never let me live it down.

Her pace quickens as if rewarding me for my answer. She's grinding against me, switching from rocking back and forth to using her knees to slide up and down me, her tits soaked in the rain bouncing with every movement.

SINISTER DESIRE

"Why?" Her question's hidden in the moaning she's trying so hard to keep quiet but failing miserably at. My hand slams over her mouth so she can free them. I want to hear everything she has but not when we could get caught by the girls.

Her eyes are back on me, sucking me into the emerald vortex behind them. There's that danger again. That worried scowl that says my answer will either hurt her or me.

I cup her breast, twisting her nipple between my fingers. If she doesn't like the answer at least she'll like what my body does to hers. "What if I said I like it?"

Her head tips back when I squeeze a little harder. "I'd ask why again."

Her answer has my other fingers between her legs, circling that spot I can still feel on my tongue, because she wants to know more. Her need to understand means she hasn't written me off. I give her part of the honest answer, "So there's one less corrupt fucker in this world."

My abs tighten as she clenches around me. I don't tell her that I revel in the moment their eyes show the realization that their time is up, that the game is over, and they're going to die because of the choices they made. I don't tell her I do it because of her.

"Fuck, Audrey. If you don't want me to—"

Her hands are on my shoulders, her weight pushing me down. I take it as a sign and grab her hips, driving into her from below. She should have stopped me because if she thinks I'm ever pulling out of her to finish, she's out of her mind.

I bite my teeth as she continues grinding on me. I don't know how she can still be coming, but she doesn't stop, even when I'm past the point of torture. I'm so sensitive, the bruises on my ribs hurt less to get.

CRUEL KINGDOMS

When she slumps over my chest, I think I actually thank God.

There's something serene about laying in the rain, my woman on top of me, both of us completely spent, our chests panting in sync. There's nothing but us shrouded in the darkness around us, cocooning us from the rest of the world.

I don't want to leave this moment, but I can't ignore the goosebumps or shiver that just ran through her. Wrapping her in my arms, I carry her back to the house. I've been up these steps enough times to know the exact spots to move swiftly, with a dead silence that wouldn't rouse a cat.

By the time I have her lying on the tiled shower, under the warm water, her eyes flutter open, reaching for the nozzle. I bat her hand away. "You'll burn."

"I like it!" She swats my hand and turns it, smiling deeper as the steam starts to rise. I don't remove the mask as I work the mud out of her hair and untangle the twigs and leaves from it. Mud, leaves, and blood cake the floor as I clean both of us off. There's a softness to her when she's in here. I noticed it the night I murdered the doctor.

Rather than ruin her peace, I wait until after I find ointment for our scrapes, after I ensure every one has been cleaned and bandaged, and after I lay her into the four-poster bed that has too many pillows, that I ask her what I've been waiting to for a year.

"Do you regret the choice you made?"

She lowers the glass of water to the nightstand, eyeing the hickey's forming down my neck and chest, the marks she made in return for the ones still healing on her. For a man who's mastered control and wields it like a weapon, I don't have any right now. Her answer is something I can't manipulate or change.

SINISTER DESIRE

My eyes are on her, studying the thoughts I can't hear, like a damn moth to a flame. I don't know if I'm seeing things as they are or how I want to, but her head shakes with confidence. "I will never regret making that choice."

My mind filters back to the last five days. To the last guard that I had beneath my hands as he begged for his life, pleading to spare him because he had daughters. It was the only time I hesitated to kill a man because it brought me back to Audrey.

"Even if it left your girls without a father?" I ask, needing to know.

Her brows pinch together. "Your choice was either I poison him myself or," she swallows, struggling to remember. Or maybe she doesn't want to.

"Poison him yourself, and I'll make myself known to you," I remind her. "Or I'll poison him for you and leave you alone."

CRUEL KINGDOMS

Little Bird

He turns to face me. The candle on my nightstand casts shadows that darken his already black attire. The top he threw on is loose and cut, showing the hickeys I made.

I don't know what's wrong with me that I'm ready for him again, that I find not only the darkness in him so appealing but everything about him, from his simple notes long ago to the fact that he's fiercely possessive in a way that's a danger to everyone but me. How he finds the humor in my outbursts, with a laugh or remark that somehow calms me down. I love that he's the only one who ever offered me a choice with a forced freedom because he just knew, like he knows everything, that I needed it. That I was too weak to make that decision myself.

"You said you liked ridding the world of corrupted people, and he was one. Richard may not have struck the girls, but he wasn't a good man." I say. "I only wished someone like you was around to poison my father or gave me the push I needed to do it myself."

His head angles, almost like he can't believe what I'm saying. I can hear the silent question repeating through the silence. Do I regret my choice—the real choice?

"No. I don't regret taking the poison you left me to kill my husband." He gave me the choice to take control of my life, and I took it. I don't know if I'm the pot or the kettle, but we're both murderers. "I don't regret wanting to know who you are." I swallow hard. "I don't regret choosing you."

The way his mask tilts, I can practically see the grin beneath, his crinkled smiling eyes hinting at it as he crawls over me, leaving a breath between us.

SINISTER DESIRE

I stop him with my hand on his chest. "But I hate you for abandoning me. For promising me that you'd show yourself, only to disappear. When you left this week…" I take a breath, hating that I let him affect me so deeply.

He leans in even more, gripping my chin and pulling me so I can do nothing but look into those deranged eyes that are filled with more promise than his actual words, "You are not lucky enough to get rid of me, little bird."

Just when I think this is the time he'll finally reveal himself, he pulls back. "You're almost ready."

When he turns to leave, my heart flutters into a strange panic that has me reaching for his hand before he's gone. I don't know or care what being ready means, but I do know that I don't want him gone from my life.

When he disappeared a year ago after promising he'd show himself, I hated myself. I felt tricked somehow. I waited for Officer Mike to arrest me for months, to come to the realization that Richard had poison in his system that caused his carriage to fall off the trail. When no arrest came, and my stalker's notes stopped, I accepted that he had abandoned me.

Seeing the note show up last week left me confused and irate. I still am. I don't know why he disappeared, and I don't know if he'll do it again.

I bring his hand to my lips as if I'm going to kiss it, and I do. He curses in pain with a twisted chuckle as my teeth sink into it first. When I look at him, I see the dark humor in his eyes, realizing what I did and why I just bit him. The hickeys weren't enough.

I promised myself that I would never be anyone's ever again, and I meant it, which is why I pull my lips between my teeth when they attempt the word, *mine*.

Chapter Ten

I sit at the edge of the fountain like every Friday morning, only this time I'm not waiting for anyone in particular. I'm cradling three gold coins in my palm and waiting for the town center to clear, trying not to focus on how ridiculous I feel for turning superstitious or how sore my entire body is after last night. We must have rolled through poison ivy because my upper back has a constant itch—of course, in the spot I can't reach either way I twist my arms to try.

I can't stop thinking about this man I don't know and yet feel pulled to at every attempt to push him away.

"Do you happen to read romance?" A throat clears next to me. "I have the newest one. Audrey, right?"

I nod before the pieces fall into place.

The girl before me is just that, a girl, not a woman. She has to be in her early twenties, and that's being generous. Her short black hair bounces on her shoulders, and her red lips make her skin glow with a dewy pale shimmer. There is a sharpness in her eyes that reminds me of Ember. A mischievous hunger. The silver ring wrapped around her right finger is simple enough. She either isn't from money, or she was married to someone who wasn't. To be a widow so young... how on earth did she get into this line of work?

SINISTER DESIRE

"I prefer mysteries." I attempt to turn away, but the girl won't take the hint. Her hand wraps around my arm with enough force to turn me back around. Facing her, I take a closer look at her this time. Her smile hasn't dropped as a shadow of a man lurks behind her. I recognize him as the threat he's meant to be.

Before last night, I would have taken that book and gone on to my usual routine, but I realize that I can't live this life forever. I don't want to. This last week, I was performing for my stalker, not these men. And before that, I was dissociating while men used my body.

My faithful follower didn't use my body; he owned it. I rode him, not because he asked or made me, but because *I* wanted to. It was this morning, when I checked my door for a note that wasn't there, that I realized I don't have to rely on any of these men. I want—no—I *desire* more for myself. Wanting insinuates I won't get it.

"Luckily, there is some mystery to it. One who starts reading romance can never truly be done." There's a threat laced into her tone that has the tall, bulky man who looks like her bodyguard take a step closer and eye me with disgust. His hand rests on the knife at his hip.

I clear my throat and take the book. "I suppose I can take a look. What does it take for someone to start hating romances?"

Her head cocks to the side with a sly grin, amused that I would ask such a question. "That's the mystery." She winks and stalks off with a bounce in her step that I want to break. I wouldn't, of course. I am not like my father.

I peek at the bookmark and frown. Everything is listed at over double the regular cost, and although I don't want to question it, something doesn't sit right. When I look back up, the two are making their way toward the church just as Mallory had a week ago.

It's the change. I don't like change. And I don't like them.

CRUEL KINGDOMS

I cradle the book in one hand and the coins in the other. I feel even more childish than I did before as I take a deep breath and mutter my wish—my prayer—to any deity who will listen, to please make it all worth it. I beg them to let me provide a better life for my girls. To grant them the gift of pure love and happiness that isn't ripped from them too soon. And before I toss all three coins, I touch my emerald and send a quick prayer that the love I lost long ago rests easy.

"It's good luck to wish with gold." My breath catches in my throat. The coins haven't even sunk to the bottom yet.

It's the woman with milky eyes who sits next to me with a warm smile. "You can call me Dove."

I take her hand in mine. "I'm—"

"I know who you are, Audrey."

I pull back, eyeing the woman closer. She's too old and blind, I think, to be the serial killer, but she is new in town, and odd. This is three times now that she's taken me off guard.

"I'm sure my reputation precedes me." I snort.

My back warms as the sun breaks the horizon and promises to roast me alive in my cloak. I want to itch, but I swear if I keep reaching for it, I'll look like I contracted something. Maybe it's Ember's words, but I'm even more paranoid that others know what I do—*did*.

"People do have a lot to say about you. A widow to a cheater who came home with another child older than yours, right? I guess *you* would have been the other woman. Did you find out before or after that poor mother died?"

I cross my arms over the book, tight against my chest. "Before."

SINISTER DESIRE

Although it's not illegal for men to have multiple wives, it's an unpracticed and frowned-upon way of living. It's always the second wife— me, in this case— who gets chastised and labeled a whore. Maybe that's why I took so easily to this lifestyle.

"And your twins, I hear they're beautiful. Why do you keep them hidden away?"

"I don't." I refute. "They've been grieving. Their father only died a year ago."

"Do *you* find it easy to grieve such a horrible man?"

My jaw drops but I quickly pick it right back up. This woman knows more than she should, and she's the first person to ever say such a thing about Richard. Everyone doted on him. "I find grieving a waste of time."

She smiles. A sight that has so many wrinkles it's off-putting paired with her youthful plush lips and round eyes. As much as her interrogation puts me on edge, there is something about her that's soft, warm, and makes me want to trust her. That's the problem with older people; they can get away with being too rude, too nice, too uncaring, and too nosy.

"But you do grieve deeply, don't you? For another?"

I halt my hand before it can reach for the emerald. He's been dead for sixteen years, so why does it feel like the universe is trying to bring him back to life by reminding me of him in some way every day?

I'm stuck in this old woman's warm blanket of questions, unable to pull myself away. I'm cemented to this stone as if I'm part of this damn fixture, mesmerized as I watch the woman take out a deck of cards from her cloak.

"I might be blind, but I see more than most do." I take the cards the woman hands me and shuffle as she instructs, handing them back when I'm done. She has me pick three and lays them facedown between us. I'm so intrigued that I prop my leg up to get a better angle, listening to her explain their meaning without having to look down at them.

"Your past is resurfacing. Whatever you've been burying deep down or trying to escape from is back, whether you are ready for it or not. Your present shows turmoil. You're doing everything for others, but it's causing harm that you aren't seeing yet. Your future holds truths. Secrets will come to light, and a stranger will make himself known sooner than you think." My stalker. "You're attending the ball, yes?"

I nod and tell her yes. I'm still not convinced she's actually blind.

I purchased all four tickets this morning, at the insistent request of my stalker, and attempted to order four new dresses, but the dressmaker refused to sell to me. Few know what I do, and the man in that store does since he's paid to offer the back room for harlot services. With the serial killer on the loose, he no longer wants to be associated with them. It was a turn of events that stumped me in my tracks because I was there not only to purchase dresses but also to ask for a job or an internship of some kind, something to start a new way of living.

I don't blame him, but it's also not going to stop me from coming back every day until he says yes.

"The ball should bring an interesting turn of events for you, but this world is a dangerous place, especially for women." The downturn in her eyes gives away her past, a haunting trauma that's branded in her forever. "Keep that knife close." Dove's head angles toward where I have a small knife tucked between my breasts.

Definitely not really blind.

She looks like she wants to say more, but a blaring scream cut through the town center, piercing our ears. Everyone's head jerks toward the church, where a woman is on her knees, her hands covered in blood, wailing, "They're dead."

SINISTER DESIRE

My feet are moving before I can think straight. My palms sweat as I follow others into the building, seeing a sight that takes my breath away. A brunette woman lay in the center of the steps with her throat slit, blood coating her naked body. A man lies next to her, naked and covered in just as much red from wounds we can't see.

I stumble back out of the church as others filter through, Officer Mike being one of them. Seeing him, I back up even faster.

Dove stops me to ask what happened. All I can tell her is that the harlot killer struck again. What I don't tell her is I know them. The dead woman is the one who accidentally knocked me over when I left that church, and the man dead at her side is the guard who attempted to assault me.

I excuse myself, hurrying away with the book clutched tight to my chest. I'm not two steps when my hand is pulled back. The old woman slips a card into my hand and walks away without a word.

I'm down the street when I see it's a note with the familiar cursive penmanship.

Throw it away.
No other man touches you but me.

Chapter Eleven

I don't have a client, but I feel dirty.

Mallory never made me feel forced into this lifestyle. Maybe, like Dove, her old age put me at ease, ignorant to any threat she held. This new girl and her bodyguard, though? They have an energy that screams chaos and not in the fun way like my stalker.

The attic stairs creak as I make the ascend. This isn't a place I visit. In fact, I keep the door shut and locked at all times so I never have to think about it. This is the first time since Richard's death that I find myself seeking it out. Outside of another shower or garden, this might be the only place I can get away from the girls' constant bickering to think clearly.

It's a mess. There's old fabric in one corner, boxes of old photos, broken dining chairs, and an assortment of other things I can't remember or place.

Tip-toeing to the window, I pull the wooden seat away to reveal my hidden stash of wine and bourbon. I'm not a drinker, but it was those long nights in this room when my husband was alive that I allowed myself to imbibe to pass the time, not whisky, though. Never whiskey.

I spot the bottle of red, pull the cork with my teeth, and swallow five long gulps before I pull it away and wince. The stale flavor leaves my tongue dry, but as long as it takes away the world for a few hours, I truly don't care how it tastes.

SINISTER DESIRE

Replacing the wood back in place, I set myself against the wall, prop my feet up, and stare out the window, taking two more pulls for the two fallen strangers who lost their lives today.

Taking the life of the guard is something my faithful follower would do, but the harlot? I refuse to believe this is his work. He cleans up after himself without leaving a trace of evidence, but I can't deny the facts. He was visibly furious when I told him what that guard attempted to do to me, and his note said that no man, other than him, touches me.

The more I think of it the harlots make sense. He wants me to stop being a harlot so he's killing them off, trying to scare me away from the job. If that's the case, I can't see him any further. It's one thing to justify the murder of corrupted men or men who harm me, but the harlots? Absolutely not.

I need someone to either shake or slap me out of this acceptance I've seemed to form about him. Harlot, guards, dollmakers, or doctors, whatever the occupation is, he's still a murderer. Then again, so am I.

It's wrong. *We're* wrong.

The last night I spent in this room replays through my mind:

My cheek burns, throbbing from Richard's reprimand. Rolling tears sting the sensitive spot even more as I pull the hidden bottle of wine from under the window seat. Richard doesn't know about my stash of liquor up here. He wouldn't allow it. Wives aren't supposed to imbibe except one glass at social parties.

That's one thing that took me by surprise when I first met him. He doesn't drink except socially and never smells of whiskey, which led me to believe he wasn't the same as my father. He's not. I'll give him that he's a better man because he hasn't laid a hand on the girls, but who's to say that won't start soon?

I won't let that happen. He would have to kill me before getting his hands on my daughters; hitting them and bruising them up like this.

CRUEL KINGDOMS

Today I met his knuckles because I attempted to nap midday, too tired and irritable from my cycle to think clearly. He waited until the girls went outside to play to remind me of my mistake and then locked me up here 'to get the quiet I so desperately require.'

I start to replace the wooden seat when a soft laugh leaves my lips, seeing the familiar paper in place of the cork.

This faithful follower, as he calls himself, has been leaving me notes for about a year now. Always in different spots around the house, but always where Richard would never look.

My hands can't unfold it fast enough to see what riddle he's left for me today—my belly lit with flame, and the smile on my face can't be more genuine.

But I let it drop to the floor the second I finish reading:

> *Tonight is the night, little bird.*
> *Either you rid yourself of this man, or I do.*
> *But the real choice is him or me.*
> *Slip the vial in his drink tonight if you wish to know who I am.*
> *If not, I'll rid you of him and me forever.*

It took me less than an hour to decide his fate. He brought a couple who were new to town over for dinner, which made it easy to slip the vial into his bourbon.

My thoughts fall to Dove, the old woman who gave me his note earlier today. I don't know how she plays into all of this, but I can't ignore that she's been around a lot, always watching me in the distance and now asking me about myself and the girls.

A familiar creak sounds from below. I jump up, my head spinning from the quick motion or maybe the wine. I make it three steps before the bottle slips from my hand and shatters at my feet.

SINISTER DESIRE

I jump over the shards and dart down the stairs. I haven't made the mistake of leaving my door unlocked again, but I know that creak.

I pull the knife out from between my breasts and peek out of the attic door. Through the small crack, I see Gus in my doorway, in the middle of either walking in or out.

"What are you doing?" I approach him, grabbing the wall when the floor sways beneath my feet. It's been a while since I felt this dizzy from booze.

His eyes fall to the knife, and I'm reminded that this is the second time he's caught me with a knife in my hand. He has to think—*know*—I'm paranoid. "Ember told me you were in here and to just walk in. I heard about Jack and wanted to check on you."

"We're fine." I prop my hand on my hip and motion toward the stairs with my chin. "Wait at the table, and I'll make you a plate."

He turns and leaves with a muttered apology. When he's gone, I step into my room to look around. Nothing looks out of sorts. I shut the door with my foot and lock it before hurrying to crouch under my bed. My shoulders drop in relief at my locked box perfectly in its place.

"How was your day?" Ember asks as we descend the stairs. The question sets alarms off in my head, but I don't know why yet.

"Fine," I say. "Did you clean your room or wash the laundry like I asked? It's your last day of chores before it's Ally's turn."

"Mhm," she hums. "You manage the tickets? The ball is in two days."

"I have all four tickets." I can't hide my in-your-face smirk. The issue is the last two dresses. I was once a part of the elite circle, so I know they'll ring me for wearing something simple, but I don't want the girls to receive the same treatment.

Ember glowers at me like I'm lying. That impish look I know too well begins lifting on her angelic face. "I want a white dress."

Of course she has demands. "To a ball? It's not a wedding."

Ember shrugs. "If I look matronly, maybe I will be one day."

This girl had never once spoken about marriage or suitors until her uncle Jack visited and put the idea in her head. It's not a bad idea, and I don't disagree with it; it's just not hers.

As much as I despise liars, I lie through my teeth and promise Ember she'll have a white dress. There isn't a chance I'll be able to swing that. White was the most expensive color because it was for a bride's wedding, not a girl for a royal ball.

I'm relieved when I find Gus didn't stay for dinner. I'm too busy to entertain visitors tonight, and we haven't seen each other since I kind of tried to seduce him when I thought he could be my stalker.

Said stalker left me physically depleted today. I barely have the energy to keep my hands up, and the twins are questioning why I'm wearing so many clothes instead of my usual house dress. I can't let them see the marks and scratches all over my body unless I want endless questions for answers I can't give.

I push him to the back of my mind even though the needle in my hand reminds me of him in ways I can't explain. Everything seems to, from the shower and the sheets to the fork I ate my eggs with this morning. Once again, he's consumed my entire life.

Dee stands on a chair, twirling the oversized sage dress, complaining, "Mother, it's huge." As if I can't see her swimming in the fabric. The two dresses I ordered last week were wrong, and since the dressmaker refused to sell me anything, I'm stuck to my own devices, pinning and piecing together this oversized monstrosity to make the perfect ball gown. At least the fabric is nice—softer and richer than the simpler ones I originally ordered.

I tell Ally to try hers on and stand on the other chair so I can work the two at once. We don't have a lot of time with the ball in only two days. Tomorrow will be filled with ballroom dance lessons, and with Ally's broken leg, everything takes twice as long.

The girls yawn, both bored of standing around and doing nothing for so long while I pin them both in place.

"I can help," Ember offers from the stairs. "Since I clearly won't be attending."

I keep my anger under control by rolling my neck and reminding myself that this time is cherished by most parents. "As I told you before, you are going, Ember. I'm getting your dress in the morning, and we'll stay up all night altering it if we need to, okay?"

I've spent the last two hours thinking about it. If the girl wants white, I'll do everything in my power to get it for her. I didn't know her mother, but I know my mother would have sold her arm to get me what I wanted, and if the roles were reversed, I would hope Ember's mother would have done the same for my girls.

"You'll be too tired to focus tomorrow. Do you want my help or not?"

I'm sure I'll regret this in less than five minutes, but I wave her over.

I was wrong; it's seven minutes before Ally screeches painfully and yells, "You did that on purpose!"

CRUEL KINGDOMS

"Ally," I inhale deeply. I know Ember did something to hurt her, but Ally really is my drama queen. She needs to learn to bite her tongue and strike back even quieter.

"Mom," the drama queen drawls out, "it's freezing in here."

At her words, a soft draft sends a chill down my spine.

On cue, all our heads turn and find the backdoor wide open. An unsettling feeling twists in my gut. "Keep working on them," I tell Ember, to my twins' absolute shock. "I'll be right back," I assure them.

They're still whining as I enter the kitchen. Nothing seems off, though it does need cleaning soon. The dishes are scattered in the sink. A load of laundry is sitting damp in the basket, waiting to be hung.

I shut the door.

The stairs creak.

As light on my toes as possible, I climb them, looking over the railing to find Ember smirking, who, without a doubt, purposely nicked Ally again.

The hallway feels darker. Every step I take feels wrong. Like I'm heading toward something I don't want to see.

Someone's up here. I can feel it.

I could take the girls and leave or call the police to inspect the house, but whoever is here would be gone by then. If it's my stalker, we aren't in danger anyway.

I don't know where that last thought comes from, considering he has murdered at least two people, maybe two more today, and likely more

SINISTER DESIRE

with how easy it is for him, but he hasn't harmed me or the girls, and I still believe he won't. He's the only man I've never felt my life at risk with.

Is this Stockholm syndrome?

I continue taking the steps with the plan to scream for the girls to run if I do find someone who isn't supposed to be here.

I'm hit with a memory that feels like a distant dream, of the boy who first showed me the excitement in the unknown—the anticipation. Like my stalker, he liked to hide and make promises too: him to keep me hidden away forever, and me swearing to never leave—we were too young to make promises we could never keep. Promises that got him killed.

I'm in the same cycle, falling for— I toss and crumple that thought aside as I push my cracked door open.

I *never* leave it open, let alone cracked.

I peer in. The candle on my dresser is flickering.

Someone is in here.

I don't get the feeling of being watched like I usually do. It's different this time. The air is grim and thick, filling me with the sudden urge to run back downstairs. I could run toward my bed and grab the knife I put there after Gus' encounter, thinking I wouldn't need it in my own house. But then what? Hope the stranger isn't a massive man I'm no match for? Hope they don't have their own weapons.

I swallow my pride and choose the first option. I start to turn away when I notice a box—*the* box—on my bed, opened.

I rush toward it.

Empty.

CRUEL KINGDOMS

My heart implodes on itself. My hands shake. My breath stops. I don't know what comes first. Fear. Terror. Longing. A loss. Grief?

My notes are gone. My bookmarks for all past encounters are gone. My money, the gold, my stalker's gifts… everything is gone.

I'm more upset than watching my daughters cry learning of their father's death; than when I learned of my father's. Maybe it makes me a bad person for holding more value in those notes, but right now, I don't care. They were mine. Aside from living for the girls' sake, they gave me something to look forward to—something *different* that pulled me from the mundane life and cracked the dull shell I was.

I take in a sharp inhale as I feel an even sharper point against my spine and another at my neck. "You missed your appointment today."

No *little bird* or dark chuckle.

This isn't my stalker. The voice is a man's but one I don't know. I don't need to know it to hear the menacing undertone. "You cost us money. We don't like losing money," he continues.

I notice then the petite dark-haired girl moving from the shadows to sit on my bed, bouncing as she lands.

"Audrey, I thought we had an understanding," her voice is sympathetic, and the way she sells it tells me all I need to know. I need to do whatever they say.

"I didn't have an appointment today." I swallow, causing the knife to knick my neck.

"You did," she coos, pulling out a bookmark from her dress. It's a different color than the one this morning. Mallory's were always the same lilac-colored marker, and the one this morning was a darker, more violet color. The one in the girl's hand right now is pink. "Right here, it says you were to meet in the back of the bakery an hour after I met with you." She tsks. "That's going to come out of your earnings."

"But—" the knife drives into my back a little harder, silencing me to let this girl finish.

"Our clients pay a lot of money, and you're one of our highest assets. You..." she laughs. "You are one of the *very* few who have zero limits. I'd even go as far as saying you are our most special asset."

Her words don't make sense. It's not like I have clients every hour, although my clients aren't simple.

The knife at my back leaves. The man's hand tightens around my mouth as he slides the flat of the other knife along my neck. He reminds me of my clients, waiting for me to do anything that gives him a reason to react, to hurt me.

"You see how easy it is for someone like you to forget an appointment and lose us money that you have to pay back? I would hate for you to end up in debt for the appointments you choose to ignore." She stands and makes a show of wiping her dress as if she sat in trash. "Show up to tomorrow's appointment, or it's those beautiful daughters of yours who will be introduced to my friend here."

She leaves out of my door, leaving me with the man at my back. Tension isn't the right word to describe how my terror thickens the air around us. His thumb traces the back of my neck until he meets fabric. I'm jerked back and hear my dress tearing quickly. All I can do is eye the bed and hope he lets go for a second, so I can run for the knife beneath my pillow.

"She's not going to be happy, but I'll let her know." He grunts with disappointment, adding a quick snicker. "Good luck with him. You're going to need it."

CRUEL KINGDOMS

    I don't understand what he means, but he tells me to wait ten minutes before I return downstairs. The first thing I do is run to my bed for the knife and grip it tight as I turn on the shower and sit in the steaming room to think. When I calm down enough, I turn around in the mirror and see what made the man tear the top of my dress.

    In the center of my upper back is a prominent C with two birds on either side of it, inked into my skin.

SINISTER DESIRE

Chapter Twelve

The foul-smelling room no longer holds the stench of death. I'm sure it's because the rats are no longer here. Although now I'm questioning how long those rats were dead and diced up before she decided to use the meat in the soup. Rats smell, but not of death unless they, well, die.

Something pulls at me to come to this room. Last night was terrifying, but those criminals didn't steal my things. The lock wasn't broken into, which meant someone had my key to unlock it. If my girls had found the box, they would have found me and asked about it.

I know Ember stole my notes. My money. My gifts. The bookmarks should be more concerning, but they were coded. She's made too many passing comments for it not to be her.

"Mom, what do you think the prince looks like?" Ally asks from the doorway, twirling her hair. "Why has he been away for so long? And why would he need to throw this ball to search for a bride?"

"I think it's to sell more tickets," Dee says with uninterest, or at least she tries to. As much as she pretends not to be into fairytales or town gossip, she always has opinions and marvels to discuss them. "The longer he waits, the more we're all willing to spend to see him. How else are royals so rich? It's that, or he's horribly ugly and couldn't find a bride on his own. I mean, why would he choose to host a ball and not have his pick of the other princesses?"

CRUEL KINGDOMS

The more she talks, I see the lights shine in her eyes as she makes her sisters dim with her "horrific" theories, as Ally calls them. "I think it's so he can walk around like a normal person, and no one would be the wiser," she suggests back.

I don't stop rummaging through Ember's closet. My excuse will be to find a dress we can alter and piece together, but my eyes are peeled for my notes. I really should be searching for a dress. With my appointment—

The clock tower chimes. My appointment is in an hour. I have to leave within five minutes, or my entire family will meet that vicious man, and I highly doubt they have a brunch in mind.

When I'm back, I'll throw together whatever I can to make the perfect dress for Ember. Something from an old birthday, a wedding, an old ball—

"Mom!"

My head hits the door, "What?"

"Have you been listening at all?" Ally stomps. "Why are you in Ember's room anyway?"

A pile of clothes is pushed to the back. I notice the light blue dress from a birthday two years prior. I let out a sigh of relief. It isn't white, but I'll be able to make it into something worthy of a ball. I pull, but it catches on something. I grab the entire pile, thrown off by the heavy weight and accidentally drop it. It lands with a loud thud. This time, when I pick it up, something tumbles to the floor.

A soft melody fills the air. The music box Richard gave her the day he died lies open at my feet.

"Yes, sorry," I call back. "The prince was at school or war or something. Royals are strange."

SINISTER DESIRE

"Imagine if the prince picked one of us to be his bride. Wouldn't that be wonderful!" Ally twirls in circles, imagining marrying a prince. And if he can make her smile the way she is now, I wouldn't argue.

"Eww." Dee's face twists in disgust. "He's double your age. You'd be better off marrying a cobbler. Brock. Or Gus!"

Ally gasps.

I pick up the music box, seeing the metal spinning without a dancer. It's not that old, but the pink fabric is torn. When I pull, it peels away easily to reveal trinkets of jewelry hidden beneath. At first glance, I think it may be Ember's mother's: a pair of dangly earrings, diamond earrings, a thin bracelet, a brown button... it's the last trinket that has my hands dropping it back to the floor. The music stops, and everything tumbles out, including a familiar emerald ring.

Chapter Thirteen

Questions fill my mind as I leave my girls and head toward town. There is something about the emerald ring that screams Mallory. It can't be hers, though. How and why would Ember have her ring? She never leaves the house. Not to mention she's a petite, blonde girl without any weight to her. There isn't a chance she could murder multiple harlots.

I don't know why I think the last question, but my mind is in a spiral.

Focus.

I need to focus. New clients are a gamble. They're unpredictable, even knowing their kink in advance. This one listed bondage, knife play, strangulation, and sensory deprivation. I'm not unfamiliar with them, but in ways that aren't listed as primary kinks. They're par for the trade in some way or another.

The bakery is closed, but I knock as instructed. Two quick taps followed by three slow and three fast.

The door opens. I enter but don't find anyone in the dark open space.

I do see the blindfold on the floor and, as the bookmark instructed, strip my clothes, hesitating before tucking my knife beneath the pile. I hate leaving it behind, but there's no place for me to hide it. All I have on is my bra and underwear before I quickly place the blindfold over my eyes.

SINISTER DESIRE

If this building were sold and rebuilt into something entirely different, this place would still have a lingering scent of freshly baked bread painted into the foundation. It's not cake that greets me now, but cinnamon and rosemary that perfume the air, probably from the rising bread on the counter someplace close by. With my eyes concealed, the scent grows stronger. I'm instantly thrown into a sense of comfort when I shouldn't be.

I hear heavy footsteps make their way toward me. I hold my breath to listen closer, smelling the air for any hints to identify this man.

A rough hand grips my arm, pulling me up to stand and leading me forward a few steps before pushing my back forward so I'm bent over a counter. Flour and sticky dough cover the wood beneath me.

A seductive tickle starts from my shoulders and runs down, toward my wrists. I hold my gasp like the expert I am when I realize it's too cold to be fingers and feels just like the blade I had against my skin last night. When he gets to my hands, he draws them behind my back, quickly securing them with tape.

I want to leave. I want nothing more but to rip this blindfold off my face and run out of this building, maybe snag a loaf of bread on the way out for my troubles. For the second time since marrying Richard, I consider running away, not just from tonight, but from this lifestyle, from this town.

That thought quickly vanishes and my survival instincts kick back in when I sense something off. I don't know what it is yet. He's not doing anything but running the knife up my arms and down my spine. He hits the tattoo my stalker gave me, and I have to bite back another whimper as the cold blade gently traces the sensitive flesh.

For my daughters. I remind myself. If I don't do this, they're the ones to pay.

CRUEL KINGDOMS

As he uses the blade to lift my chin, I realize this could be the serial killer. He could so easily slice me up and leave me for dead. Another harlot off the streets, corrupting the town's men.

No. The killer poisons their victims. I haven't eaten or drank anything, so how would they poison me? I answer my own question immediately: needles, force feed me, poison on a rag; the possibilities are endless.

He presses against me from behind, and replaces the blade with his hand, gripping my chin to pull my neck back. "I know you." The voice is too distorted to recognize it.

I don't respond. The men who are into these kinks use any excuse to cut or strangle me for their pleasure, whether I speak or stay silent. And since it wasn't a question, I assume he doesn't want a response.

It isn't odd that this person knows me. Most do. I'm the widow of a very influential man. I used to host parties on a weekly basis. Not many people don't know me in this town. The meaning behind his words feels different, though.

"Do you like being a harlot?"

I swear I'm about to die. I swallow the fear down and pretend it's two weeks ago when I wouldn't think twice about being tied up, blindfolded, or bent over for a stranger.

"What's not to like?" I tease in my usual breathy way while wiggling my ass. I need to get a grip and find the old Audrey before it costs me my life. The Audrey who pretends she wants to be here. Like whichever man before me is the most important one in the world.

"No!" His voice is tight. His hand lowers to wrap around my neck. I force myself to recognize this as a kink and not a threat to my life. "I don't want those rehearsed responses. I want a real answer. Do you *like* this job?"

SINISTER DESIRE

"No," I answer honestly. "But there are necessary evils in this world."

His breath is hot on my ear. "Do you think I'm evil?" I don't ignore where the knife points against my ribs. One strong push and it'll hit my heart.

"I think people are evil, but what we like sexually isn't. I signed up for this, so no, you aren't evil for doing what you want and what I allow. What's evil is the people who threaten my life, my family, in order to get me here."

I bite my tongue. I said too much.

His hand loosens around my neck, letting his finger trail and push against where my pulse throbs. I don't move or dare say anything else while I wait for him. He wants answers, to understand, but more importantly, he wants control.

It's always about control—power.

The more seconds that tick by, I honestly think this might be the harlot killer. I only know one murderer, and he's giving off the same dense energy of either having killed or having an urge to.

"What do you want?" he asks, calmer now.

I feel him press at my entrance, so I give him the response they all want. "You."

He pulls away and the knife is back at my throat. I hold my breath and feel tears pool my lash line. "To be free," I answer quickly. The knife falls, allowing me to speak better. "I'd let you kill me now to be free if I knew my family was happy and safe." I sniffle, but the words leaving my mouth are like a broken faucet. "I wish I could say something as typical as love or money or fame, but I've had them all. The only one of them worth a damn was love, and I'm not talking about the love for your children or parents, either. I mean real, unique, infatuated, borderline obsessive love. Where the word love feels stupid to say because the feeling is too strong. I want…" I pause because it's impossible. I want not to feel things for my stalker the same way I did for Charming. "I don't want to lose someone like that again."

I lay my head against the counter weakly. Let him cut me or strangle me. I'm too numb to care. The memories I buried deep are at the forefront of my mind, taunting me. The very scent in the air is a reminder of him.

"Your husband?" He's lined up again as if it is a reward for answering honestly.

"No." I don't hesitate. "I was sold to him when I was fifteen. He cheated on me, beat me, and locked me in the attic for a total of three years. I counted because what else can you do locked in a room for weeks and months on end?" I start to laugh and I don't know why.

"Who then? A lover? You had an affair?"

"We were young. I didn't even know his name before he died." A grieving grin threatens my lips. He wasn't charming in the slightest, but I called him it anyway to get a rise out of him. He didn't call me anything but Audrey, with that cold voice that warmed as the days passed.

The man at my back pushes into me, stretching me slowly. With how big he is mixed with the vulnerable emotions I left on the counter, I'm too sensitive, flesh and soul. I want to run away but I let him take me. The pain in my chest is almost worse than the way I feel like I'm betraying my stalker in some way.

I hate myself right now. I hate myself for feeling the way I feel for another man I don't know.

SINISTER DESIRE

"What do you want?" I cry out as he sinks all the way in. "You're very specific on your listed kinks. Is it pain? Tears? Vulnerability? Do you like watching women break?"

He retreats, and just when I think he's about to pull out, he pulls away my blindfold and drops the mask beside my head, driving into me again with a kiss on my neck.

"I want you, little bird." His voice changes to one I know. He pauses for a breath, then continues as I nearly cry in relief. "The kinks were to get on *your* card. I bought the whole thing out to see if you'd show."

I feel something cold slide between my cheeks before pressure fills the hole he's not in. "Relax, little bird. I'm just claiming every piece of you. Ridding you of every man that's been here before me." He kisses my neck again as the pressure builds. My toes curl. It doesn't hurt, but kind of. None of the men I've been with have wanted anal; there was another girl who took those men. It's a feeling that's almost indescribable and yet the most describable feeling every human being knows, but no one would dare speak out loud.

I want to tell him he's the first, but knowing he's enjoying the claim helps me relax, even as the tape digs into my wrist.

He must sense my discomfort because the tape is cut away, freeing my hands to brace myself on the counter.

"I told you to get rid of that damn book." He lets out a heavy breath like he's disappointed in me. "I said no other man was to touch you, and you showed up here anyway?"

I try to regulate my breathing as he fills me with different rhythms I can't focus on. "I left the book in my safe. Even if I threw it away, they would have shown up and threatened me and my family. If I knew it was you behind it all—"

CRUEL KINGDOMS

"It wasn't me," he says as he pulls out and lines himself up to replace his fingers.

I wiggle away. "You'll tear me in half!"

His dark chuckle is like downing a glass of wine. "Do you trust me?"

Yes. I hate that I do, but I nod the best I can with my head against the counter.

"The people who threatened you were from another kingdom. The harlot operation you work for is a lot larger than you think." His fingers run down the tattoo on my spine. "They should have seen this and known."

"He did," I say as he slowly tears me in fucking half.

"I need you to relax." His kissing and sucking on the back of my neck starts to relax me, but damn, it's hard to focus on that with the other foreign feeling behind me. My breaths are choppy as he runs his fingers down my hair, trailing down my ribs. His tongue on my skin is what does it.

Heat fumes my body as he drives all the way in. I'm so happy he does because I couldn't take any more of the slow, patient agony.

I know he wants details. Tonight showed me a whole other side of my stalker. A deeper side that, now that I know it was him, solidifies that I'm a maniac for having any sort of feelings for him.

Stockholm syndrome. That's what we're calling it. And I'd gladly walk into the psych ward if it meant keeping him.

I tell him about the entire interaction, how the man tore my dress and told me he'd *tell her*, then demanded I wait ten minutes before going back to my daughters.

SINISTER DESIRE

He tenses. A reaction that quickly vanishes as he touches the C at the top of my back, promising me they won't bother me ever again. I don't ask if he plans to kill them because I truly don't care. They threatened me and my family.

I do ask him if he killed the guard, which he answers with a swift "No," as if he's annoyed he didn't get to.

He grips my hips tighter and starts to move inside of me. His fingers come around to my nipple, splitting my attention between the different titillating sensations.

My legs are useless, and it's getting harder to keep my feet steady on the ground as the blood rushes to my head, making me dizzy.

The mask beside me disappears.

He pulls out of me, his weight vanishes, and without him pinning me in place, my knees give out. He grabs me before I can fall, lifting me so I'm on the edge of the counter, pulling my hips, and lifting my knees so he's lined up again.

The moan that leaves me matches his grunt as he sinks back in, easier this time, using short, shallow thrusts to tease out the strange pleasure. I don't know what comes over me, but my hands fall between my legs, working myself as he does, circling that spot that has him cursing at the sight.

"Yours," I groan as my body bursts to life. When he told me he was mine in the garden, I didn't deny or accept it because the fact that he made me come harder than I ever had before confused the hell out of me. I've never wanted to be anyone's again, but I can't deny this pull toward this man. I'm not giving my body to anyone else's, so if he wants to claim me, I'll let him.

CRUEL KINGDOMS

When his low chuckle behind the mask hits my ears, his hands tighten around my thighs, and he moves in and out of me at a torturing, elongating pace, I know exactly what he's thinking.

He truly does get anything he desires.

SINISTER DESIRE
Faithful Follower

She's ready.

I thought losing five days with her would set me back, but it seems to have done the opposite. Physically, we were never going to be an issue, but it's more than that; she trusts me.

When I saw her standing there with the blindfold, I almost lost it. Not only did she show up when I told her no one else was to touch her, but she left her fucking knife on the ground, leaving her completely defenseless—with a serial killer targeting people who do the very thing she's there to do.

My natural instincts kicked in and I grabbed the discarded knife, waving Duke to get out of there because the plan had changed. A much less terrifying one for her. Duke frowned at not being able to scare the shit out of her. He had his mask ready, a beast-like face which gives even me the creeps.

The plan was to scare her into never considering taking another client again, just in case she hadn't come to that conclusion on her own, but my specialty is interrogations.

I took the knife and decided to ask some questions, starting with why she showed up. Everything snowballed from there. *Charming's* death having a hold on her didn't stop her from giving herself to me, admitting that she's mine.

I'm so fucking happy I marked her. I know the harlot operation is larger than this town, but we haven't been able to pinpoint who runs it.

CRUEL KINGDOMS

Whoever the man is who threatened Audrey is high enough in power that he saw the marking and knew better than to touch her.

The dress shop is closed like the rest of the town, but Duke unlocks it and slips in easily enough. My little bird might have been turned down, but I won't be. I saw the girl's dresses when I slipped in last night. They're too stunning to replace. It's only her that needs one.

I'm tossing through the different colors until I find the one I'm looking for. It's Dove headed toward me that makes me pause and turn. The annoyed look on her face can only mean one thing.

"Your sister is here."

I don't have to ask which one. Eva keeps to herself and is too preoccupied with training for the revenge that she thinks I don't know about.

The other one? She's too close to our father, his right-hand woman, who's better than anyone I know at integrating herself into others' lives and seducing their biggest secrets from them.

My problem with her isn't with her skills or the fact that I don't truly trust her; it's that the woman is cursed. I swear, every place she goes, trouble follows. There hasn't been a ball she's attended that hasn't ended in some sort of disaster, whether she's involved or not.

"Be sure she stays away from Audrey."

I don't want anything or anyone to ruin when I reveal myself to my little bird tonight.

Chapter Fourteen

I can't sit down as I finish the alterations on the girl's dresses.

I don't remember getting home. My faithful follower was pulling my hips back into him when I passed out. I do remember silently yelling at him for branding me when he laid me on my bed after showering me *thoroughly*. He showed me the prominent bite mark between his thumb and forefinger and said I started it before correcting himself because, apparently, he gave me my tattoo the night of my birthday.

"What is that?!" Ember shrieks as a plate shatters on the ground. "Is that my old dress? You went into my room?!"

"Yes," I tell her, finishing up the final touches. It's taken me all day to piece together the pale blue fabric with a few additions from my old dresses. The boning in the corset is breathable, so she can eat and drink freely tonight. If I'm honest, it's remarkably more beautiful than the girls' dresses, and a prickle of pride fills me. If I can show this to the dressmaker, he would have no choice but to hire me.

Ember crosses her arms, and I know I'm about to get a headache. "It's not white."

"The carriage will be here soon." I ignore her remark and toss the dress to her. "Be ready within an hour."

Without another word, she stalks up the stairs and slams the door, twice.

CRUEL KINGDOMS

While I wait on the girls, I quickly put myself together as much as I can. My hair is curled, my makeup is thick, and my dress is simple. When I look in the mirror, I see my mistake; I look like a harlot readying for an afternoon tea, not a royal ball. I clean my makeup and restart to make it more subtle.

I'm no longer a harlot, I remind myself.

When I turn to make my way downstairs, I notice a long white box waiting on my bed. My door is closed, but my window is slightly cracked. I fly across the room to grab the note perfectly centered on top of it, finding another game he wants to play: The King says.

The King says you're ready. Wear this and meet me in the courtyard at midnight.

Inside is a blood-red dress with a hint of violet stitching under the bosom. The sleeves are off the shoulder and bring attention to the emerald around my neck. The skirt isn't excessive like most prefer but gives the perfect volume to accentuate my waist. I shouldn't be, but I'm slightly surprised, and my insides tickle with a dreadful pleasure that he knows I would hate something so extravagant. It's the girls' night, not mine.

Beneath the soft dress are four masks. I hadn't even considered the ball would be a masquerade. It makes me wonder what else I missed.

A prickle of excitement eats at me to find out what he's been readying me for.

A knock comes from the backdoor. As I cross the house to answer, I hear the girls talking about their recent day with Lucy and Brock. The happiness in their voices softens my heart to a useless sponge in a way that only they can. Ember's room is quiet, but I change my mind to check on her when the knocking grows louder and more demanding.

SINISTER DESIRE

"Girls, the carriage is here," I call out, but when I open the door, it isn't a footman.

"Jack? What are you doing here? I told you—"

He shoves past me and takes a seat at the head of the table. "Where is Ember?" He kicks his feet up and lights a cigarette. His eyes rake up and down the new dress like a starving dog salivating after a piece of steak. It's not a compliment. This man has looked at me like this since the day I met him, and I am sure he would look at a nice meal the same way. He's someone who starves and yearns for the things he can't have.

"Uncle Jack! Finally." Ember rushes toward him and kisses his cheek. When she turns to me, my blood is boiling. As her wicked smile lifts even higher, I recognize the severe loathing rushing through every inch of my skin, the sleeping viper who stirs with a need to retaliate. I'm at my breaking point. If she were next to me, I might have actually hit her.

She did find her white dress after all.

My fists shake at my side as I see the wretched woman wearing my mother's wedding dress. The one she made but never wore, swearing that one day we would make it away from my father and she would find a man she would wear it for. One she truly loved. It wasn't the most beautiful, but it was hers. It was *mine*.

Ember drops the pale blue dress, cut into shreds, onto the dining room floor. If I weren't already simmering with rage, I would be seeing all my work destroyed in a matter of seconds.

"What are you doing, Ember?"

"I told you I wanted a white dress. It's not like you were going to wear it anytime soon." She giggles as Jack plops a stack of papers onto the table. "Uncle Jack here learned something interesting. It seems this house belongs to me."

CRUEL KINGDOMS

"Not until you marry." I didn't want to tell her this because I'm sure she'll marry the first man off the street to have something over me, but I'm done with her and her antics. If she wants to be miserable, let her. I'll take my girls someplace else, start new if we have to. "Technically, it goes to the next man in your father's bloodline. There is none. I know where you're going with this, and if your Uncle Jack did have any rights over it, it was forfeited the second he was arrested, again, and again, and again. And if you marry, it's your husband's estate, not yours."

I expect her to huff with frustration, but I should know better than to expect anything from her. The look she's giving me is unsettling at best, and the way she twirls her blonde curls with her fingers reminds me that I'm not dealing with someone who is reasonable. My eyes shift to Jack, who's giving me the same amused look. Like they know something I don't.

With the way the chandelier is dully lit, the shadows around the room bring forth an ominous energy that's making this exchange chilling. Alarms are ringing in my head that something isn't right.

"Her father did take out her dowry, but we found something much more interesting in your possession." Jack leans back farther into the chair while Ember skips out the door, comes back with a box, and dumps it on the table.

I see my stalker's notes, the jewelry he gifted me, the bookmarks, and the last book. I should have gotten rid of them instead of keeping them like trophies. The bookmarks were coded, but I should have burned them like I used to. Ever since the stalker's notes started, I kept them, thinking maybe he could be one of them, circling the ones I considered he could be, then the ones he showed himself at.

He threw off my routine. The change is what caused my slip-ups. Made me sloppy.

SINISTER DESIRE

"You had me fooled for a while," Ember starts again, taking a seat next to her uncle. "But then I found all of this. You claim we don't have money, but you hide bags of gold and jewelry. You managed tickets to the ball that cost a fortune. How can a whore manage all of this? Is it your lover? Is that what these notes are?"

I don't explain myself. My lips are tight, my arms are folded in front of me, and my chin is high, like someone who's waiting for a tantrum to be over.

"I found someone who was able to tell me what these bookmarks say." My heart hammers, but I'm an expert at controlling my reactions when I need to. I don't so much as blink. "The code in them." Ember's eyes lighten with a new satanic glimmer as she cackles. "I can't believe you let men do these things to you."

Jack eyes me again, and I don't miss the way he shifts in his chair before speaking. "Here's how this is going to work. You're all going to the ball as planned, and you'll be back with as much money as you gather before the clock strikes midnight. And if you're not, I'll call our dear friend Officer Mike and tell him about your list, exposing you and those men. I'm sure the palace guards will walk away with a slap on the wrist, but you? You'll be cast out, and the girls will be shunned for having a whore mother."

My brain isn't working fast enough. I clock every movement he makes as his feet come off the table, and he stands, heading towards me.

"Why tonight?" I ask as his tobacco stench reaches my nostrils first. He leaves no space between us as he hovers over me. Now that he knows things about me that he shouldn't, he is a little more intimidating than usual. His height is impressive, and for the first time, I'm sizing him up as the threat he's slowly becoming. "Give me more time, and I'll find a way to get you the money you want."

If it's money they want for their silence, that should be easy enough to manage. I'll sell my last dress if I have to, and as much as I don't want to,

CRUEL KINGDOMS

I'd revert back to being a harlot. I can't go to jail and leave my girls without any parents.

A knock pounds on the door. I meet Jack's eyes, and he sees the idea hit me. In one quick motion, his fist strikes my temple before I can react. Tiny black stars fill my vision, but he catches me before I can fall, bringing my back against his chest. His hand reeks of cigarettes as he covers my mouth. I struggle, but my head is pounding, and I can't breathe with his hands so tight on my face.

He drags me behind the door as Ember opens it.

Gus storms in. "Sorry, I'm late."

Hope fills my chest, seeing the massive man standing in the middle of my kitchen. I scream as loud as I can against Jack's palm and kick anything I can with my feet, stomping hard on the ground. He spins around and I see the confusion on his face as he takes in my captured position against Jack.

"What's with the dramatics?" His eyes land on Jack. "It's not like she's going to fight you. She wouldn't want us to hurt her girls. Oh, wait," He nods toward me. "She does like to keep knives on her."

I don't believe what I'm hearing. I couldn't have heard him correctly, or maybe I didn't understand. The world around me dims—implodes.

Gus hugs Ember before pulling her face in for a kiss. "You look beautiful. The keys I copied work, I see." He eyes the table.

"Thank you." She twirls for him, kisses him again, and turns to me with a wicked grin. "Do you think he would really come around once a month to check on the house of a whore? He was coming to see me."

SINISTER DESIRE

Jack pulls my hands, keeping them secured in one hand as his other hand roam up and down my sides, searching for the knife. I jerk but fail as his hold tightens, "I don't have it! I left it under my pillow."

He continues his roaming, groping under my breasts. He pauses with a snicker before his hands plunge down my neckline, touching more than he needs to before finding it tucked between my breasts.

When he lets me go, I can't find words to say or ask. Without the knife, I have nothing, can do nothing but watch the three of them with utter shock. Then I remember Ember is still a girl and with only my voice as my weapon, I ask, "Why were his hands all over me last week?" I eye Gus with a feigned betrayal that I feel for different reasons.

"He told me you got him drunk and threw yourself at him!" Ember sneers. It's only when Gus places his hand on her shoulder that she visibly relaxes into him, but there's still doubt in her eyes. She shakes her head as if to rid herself of a thought. "The house is mine if I marry. So, I guess I'm trying to tell you this is your last night here." She holds her hand out and reveals the band around her finger, pulling Gus' to show off his next. "The papers will go through by tomorrow."

"Consider your rent due by midnight," Jack chuckles at my back. "The back pay you should have been paying my niece for the last year. You get that tonight, you can leave, and we'll stay silent."

"Gus thinks you'll use your body to get the money, and Jack thinks you'll resort to stealing what you need to. I think you won't make it in time, and we get to sell the twins." Ember laughs as she saunters toward the counter and pulls a knife from the block.

My throat dries. I was gone too much not to have noticed this. I'm piecing together things that are too late. Ember knows what I do but she knew before that box was unlocked. Her etiquette is horrible, so she certainly hasn't been attending any of the classes; she's been following me.

CRUEL KINGDOMS

Gus has been here more than I realized and Jack, too. The twins were too busy with their classes and did everything to stay out of her way to notice.

The twins' voices and heels greet us before their presence. They gush with excitement as they rush through the arched doorway. It's Gus who moves, grabbing Ally as she walks through first.

I jump forward, but my arm is yanked back, pulling me against Jack as his fist strikes my temple in the same spot. I know it's bleeding by the white horror on Ally's face as she squeals and jerks in Gus' hold.

Ember holds the knife out toward Dee, who looks to me for help.

Help I can't provide. I've never felt so helpless or cursed. If I have to watch the last people I love die, I'll follow after them this time.

"We're keeping this one as collateral. In case you get any ideas about skipping town too soon." Gus says, tossing Ally into a chair, awkwardly with the cast on her leg. She has enough sense in her to stay still and quiet.

"I'll keep a close eye on Dee tonight while you *mingle*." Ember holds the knife closer to Dee's throat, whose hands are up in surrender, keeping one eye on her sister. If Ally weren't in trouble, Dee would jump on this girl without a care if she gets cut in the process, but not with a threat of Gus at her sister's back.

"They can both come. I'll get you the money!" I'm shouting. I can't leave Ally… I… my thoughts are spinning too fast. I have no choice.

Ember rounds Dee and pushes her out the door, motioning for me to follow them. I have no arguments to give. Nothing I say will change their mind.

My legs are like mud as I attempt to walk behind them when I'm pulled back. The door shuts, and I'm slammed against it. "What does your lover call you? Little bird?" Jack's tobacco breath is hot on my face again. "If you don't come back with the money. I'll be sure to use you in every fucking way I can before I call the cops. And while you may be used to it, I don't think your girls are. Gus is a big guy, *little bird*."

Chapter Fifteen

The palace sits far back, down a long winding road. From town, its towers and turrets peak in the distance, but seeing it up close is something else entirely. I wouldn't be surprised if there were a secret town hidden behind these walls.

I push away my awe and remember my one goal for the night, the only thing that should be on my mind: collect as much money as I can. I don't believe it's the money they're after, but they have Ally, and I can't think about anything else right now.

Sneaking away to round back to the house isn't an option either, not with Dee at Ember's side and Gus waiting outside the gates to ensure we don't attempt to run away.

Finding my stalker before midnight to ask him for help would be ideal, but he wants to meet at midnight, not before. I'm not even sure how to find him in the crowd of masks. Most of them are half-faced masks, sparkling, laced, feathered, or plain. There are so many people, and although the vaulted ceiling and vast space provide a semblance of space, the massive dresses make the room more crowded than necessary.

Finding my stalker is next to impossible. I have to rely on myself.

Gus was right, I'll use my assets the only way I know how to. I'm not a thief. I've never stolen anything in my life and testing it out in a heavily guarded castle isn't a smart move.

SINISTER DESIRE

Dee grasps my hand and looks up at me, and I know exactly what she's thinking without her having to say a word. Ally would love this place. The royal luxury, the glamorous gowns, the elegant music, it's all from one of her fairytales. Instead of dancing around the ballroom or admiring the smallest detail, like the enormous diamond chandeliers or golden candelabras, she's alone with Jack, scared for her life and waiting for me to save her.

The guard takes the red invitations and offers me a wink. Either he greets everyone this way, or he recognizes me under the red glittering mask. My green eyes and emerald necklace probably give me away.

At any other time, I might have recognized him or tried to, but my head is pounding from where Jack struck me twice. Mentally, I'm tucking him in the back of my mind as an option to round back to if I need it.

I gladly accept the champagne flute offered to me as we make our way around the ballroom, grabbing another when the server turns her head. I need all the courage I can get tonight. I toss the first one back and sip on the second one as if it were my first.

Dee is pulled from my hand. "Tick Tock, Audrey," Ember says as she leads her away. I can't argue or make a scene. I'm forced to watch as they make their way toward the food and start mingling with others their age. My daughter paints the perfect smile on her face, and if I didn't know any better, I would assume nothing was amiss. She might be her father's twin, but her personality and adaptability are all mine. If it were her in that house with Jack, I wouldn't be as worried.

"Lady Audrey, what a surprise!" A familiar voice comes from behind me and pulls me away, snapping away my protective gaze to meet her assessing one. Her jaw is wide open as she takes in my dress. "You've come up quickly. That dress is exquisite. Where did you get it?"

CRUEL KINGDOMS

I've attended parties with this woman many times. A socialite gossip who, I admit, used to find enjoyable, always offering insight into a world I wasn't born into. In the end, none of the women offered anything but a letter of condolences and a few somber faces after my husband died.

Like Dee, I plaster on my best smile and heighten my voice to tell her it's a secret I refuse to give up. Her eyes become saucers, filling with a hunger to know more. I don't know how I ever found her delightful when I find her so detestable now.

"Maybe you can tell me more when you bring the girls over. My boys are back from boarding school in a few days."

This is why I wanted to attend this night. I need this connection and any others I can swing. I want my daughters to have options that I didn't. If they want a baker or a shoe cobbler, I truly don't care, but I want them to have all the choices they can get in this world without concern for money or status.

"They would love that!" I meet her excitement. "I just have to meet someone right now. I'll stop by next week?" I don't wait for her reply to zig-zag through the crowd and find a wall. The last thing I want is to get lost in gossip with a gabber like Hannah.

Most of the guests are gathered around the center to dance, though how they manage with the massive skirts is beyond me. That was something I could never fake interest in—the gowns or dancing.

"Crowds aren't your thing either?" I turn and find a woman wearing a sleek black dress and black mask with tiny points, almost like horns, standing next to me. Her blonde hair is uniquely light and waves down to her waist. Her eyes are taking me in as a man would, and I can't stop the flush that ignites under her tempting gaze. I don't need to see her face to know she's stunning.

SINISTER DESIRE

My smile lifts naturally. She's holding an empty flute while tossing back the second one.

"I like crowds just fine," I say. "At this angle."

I know I should leave to focus. To find a man and take him into a dark room, but I like this woman's energy. I'm drawn toward her for reasons I can't explain.

"The last ball I went to was a disaster." The woman laughs, showing her perfect teeth and a sharp dimple that makes my head spin. "Are you from this Kingdom or the neighboring ones?"

"This one."

"You're not one for chatter either." She chuckles and grabs two more flutes off a passing server, handing me one. "Loosen up a little. I tried to get them to put strawberry garnishes on them, but my brother refused."

I look at the drink and then the woman again. An idea forming with technicalities that might not fill me with so much guilt.

Taking her advice, I relax my shoulders and face her. "Are you married?" I ask, slipping my fingers beneath her strap to right it, letting them linger along her collarbone a little longer than polite.

The woman's eyes are magnificent. A mix of hazel and violet. Her teeth peek again when she drags her bottom lip in. Her hand slides over mine and I notice her nails are sharp, shimmering, deep purple points. "How much?"

My heart flutters. I'm not even offended. I'm throwing myself at her like the harlot I have to be tonight. "A lot."

The woman chuckles again, and it's the sultriest sound I've ever heard. Cupping my hand into hers, she pulled me down a hall, then another. She must know the layout of this place and is looking for a specific room. One she finds after two more turns.

The room is too dark to see anything, not that I have time to look around. The second the door clicks, the woman's hands are in my hair. She spins us, and my back hits the door. My head aches, but I don't pay attention when the taste of champagne and blackberries hits my tongue.

I've never kissed a woman. It's softer and seductive.

"I have *a lot*." Her giggle tickles my neck, and damn if it doesn't have me feeling things I shouldn't. I don't know if it's her taste, or how she's melting into me, or the fact that it's something I shouldn't be doing, but my body is reacting in ways I didn't expect. She spins us again, and this time, I fall back onto a bed. "I pay for discretion. Name your price. Any price. And it's yours."

Her hands are even softer on my legs as she leans over me and kisses down my neck.

My ears are ringing by the time her fingers pull down the neckline of my dress and tease my taut nipple.

"She's not for you, Mel."

That deep, distorted voice brings me out of whatever trance this woman has me in. I didn't even hear the door open.

Wait, he called her by name? How does he know her?

"Come on…" she whines, climbing off me. "Don't ruin my fun." She pauses. "Or hers."

I can hear the glower behind his mask. A mask I don't see but know is there. "She's *mine*."

SINISTER DESIRE

"I had her first." There was a new attitude in Mel's voice. A woman marking her territory. "And don't give me the '*I'm a trained killer*' threat either. We all know your body count is higher than the plaque."

I sense movement before I feel his hands on me. He flips me on my stomach and, with expert speed, unties my dress. I know what he's doing before I hear Mel's resigned sigh. "This is her?" Another pause. "You're such a romantic sadist."

I turn to sit up, adjusting myself. Mel's lips are on me before I get a chance to stand. "Find me when you get bored of him."

I imagine her winking as she walks out of the dark room, leaving me alone with my faithful follower.

How did you know I was here? The question is almost out when I remember he's a stalker—*my* stalker. He knows everything.

My eyes finally adjust enough to make out his outline. He's wearing formal wear, and his hands are in his pockets. His mask is no longer the black one but a matching blood-red mask to mine, without the glitter.

"I said no other man touches you."

I cross my arms. "You didn't say women."

His head drops and shakes with a soft chuckle that shakes his shoulders. He takes one step toward me, pausing to leave two steps between us. It's the first time I've seen him hesitate as he lifts the mask away, tossing it to the side.

My heart drops to my stomach.

The pieces I've been collecting all fall into place. He was handsome then, but now? Devastatingly beautiful.

CRUEL KINGDOMS

His jaw is just as stubborn and tight as when I first met him the night I ran from my father and hid in a pumpkin patch, bleeding and dying. His sharp cheekbones and deep chocolate eyes hold a similar intensity he had when I woke from my allergic reaction. Only now, they belong to someone who has seen and done too much. The boy who stitched me back together grew up to make his own wounds in others—*a trained killer*, Mel said.

His raven hair is shorter now but suits him better. It takes away the boyish features that he never really had. There was always a coldness in him that I wanted to warm. A smile that only lifted when he succeeded at scaring me or getting me to talk about things I thought I never would.

I glance at the rest of him, merging the ghost of a boy and the angelic demon of a man in front of me. He has the faintest scar on the back of his hand, his palms are callous, and he has a shadow of stubble along his face. There is an imperfection through one of his dark brows, a scar, but I can't focus on it when I realize he's staring at me.

Those dimples…

His face splits into a grin that leaves my knees too weak to stand, my throat too dry, and my head spinning. The second those dimples show I think I'm hallucinating. "Charming?"

He's older but I would never be able to forget his face. I couldn't if I tried.

"How…" my voice cuts off, and I have to clear my throat. "You're dead!"

I watch his grin fall to a tormented frown. "No, bird, you were."

I don't understand what he's saying. My knees are finally too weak to keep me standing, and I'm lucky the bed is behind me when I fall back while gripping my aching head. "How is this possible? I saw... I saw your burning body."

He lowers next to the mattress, and I almost jump back to my feet, convinced it's a ghost sitting next to me. It doesn't feel real. This boy, who's a man now, hid me away and gave me the best five days of my life—until we were found, and everything went to hell.

"My father told me you were dead," he starts. His voice is no longer distorted by the mask, and I can see the rest of his face match the emotions he shows through his eyes so clearly. "After your father dragged you back home, I told my father we needed to find you, that he'd hurt you again. He told me I was being an idiot child and sent me away to a private school. Made me join the military. I escaped once to come back and find you, but he said you died. He showed me the grave." I follow every word he says like my life depends on it. "I planned to stay away forever, but I couldn't let go. I fell into a group where I met someone who finds people who don't want to be found. You met her, Dove. She sent me the article about your husband having multiple wives and the scandal it was causing in this town, and she had the photo of you and the twins."

I remember that article. It was the day I stopped liking Hannah. She had found the letters from Ember's mother, stole them, and passed the gossip around faster than wildfire.

"My father showed me your burned corpse," I say, reliving my worst memory. "He... he had your necklace." I lift my hand to the emerald around my neck. It's on a different chain now, but it was his. I remember my knees hitting the pebbles when I saw the dead body—can still feel them embedded in my skin from how hard I fell.

We both thought the other one to be dead all these years.

"I lost it. He must have found it and—"

"And murdered a different boy?" I ask. "Why? Why go through all that trouble?"

I'm staring into the dark eyes of the boy I loved years ago. My stalker. My *faithful follower*.

A memory hits me at the sight. It wasn't of him chasing me around a room, hiding under a bed, or looking for him with anticipation that he would jump out at any second, or doing ridiculous things he says just because, "The King says." I've always remembered playing childish games for days, talking endlessly, and eating the most delicious food I've ever had. What I didn't remember was those first two days, I was in and out because of my allergic reaction. I can hear him now, though, promising that no one would take me from him. That I was *his* little bird.

"His reasons don't matter. He's not taking you from me again." His hands cup my neck as he pulls me in. "I wanted to do this for so long without that fucking mask. With you knowing."

His lips meet mine, and it's different knowing who he is. Better. I thought I would die, never knowing this feeling again. I lean in, pulling myself deeper into him, my hands clutching his lapels as his tongue teases mine. I'm lost—entranced—my mind muddled when his finger brushes my temple and I jerk back in pain, remembering why it hurts.

I hate myself for pushing him off. I hate myself for dragging him into my mess, but he's the only one I can think of asking. "I don't want to stop, I have so many questions, but I need your help."

"Anything." His thumb brushes along my temple again, his brows furrowing when I whimper. "But first, who the fuck hurt you?"

I'm crying now. The weight of everything settles deep inside of me. This whole situation, my life—our lives—were a disaster.

SINISTER DESIRE

He leans in and kisses me again, "Tell me what's going on, Audrey." His eyes are searching now, trying to read me for any information. I tell him everything, as much as I can, in less than five minutes. His hand on my knees anchors me from breaking down completely.

When I'm finished, he stands, pulling me up with him. "It'll take a minute to get what I need." He opens the door, but I stop him, reminding him I have to find Dee first. I can't leave her here with Ember.

His hand tightens around mine like he doesn't want to let me go, but time is running out. "Find Dee. I'll need twenty minutes, but I'll have everything we need to get Ally and—" He pauses. *Kill them* left unsaid. "Just wait for me outside the gates." As much as I don't want to, I agree and turn.

My hand is yanked back before I can make it one step, my body hitting his as his lips meet mine. His body caves around me, deepening the kiss. By the time he pulls away, my head is dizzy, and my body is melting for more.

He lets go and with his hand on the small of my back, pushes me out the door first. "While you're gone, please try not to kiss my sister again."

I gasp and face him. His dimples are on full display as he tucks his hands into his pockets and turns the other way down the hall.

Mel was his sister? And I almost…

By the time I find my way back to the ballroom, the prince's dance has begun. A familiar white dress twirls around the floor. I move closer and squint my eyes to be sure, confirming it's Ember in the arms of a handsome man as everyone looks at them with loving eyes.

"Mom!" Dee whisper-yells and hurries toward me. "The prince picked Ember and dragged her off. "We should go back and get Ally while she's distracted!" She threads her arm into mine and pulls.

CRUEL KINGDOMS

I follow, letting her lead the way. As we near the door I stop her, lowering to her level so she understands how serious I am. "Lucy doesn't live far from here, right? I need you to take a carriage to her house. Don't come home. I'll come get you when it's over. Do you understand?"

My daughter's chest rises too quickly. She senses my fear, and I need her to. I ask her again if she understands, shaking her shoulders to get a grip on herself. She nods.

The rain's coming down hard as we head toward the waiting carriages. I'm too focused on them to care about the man trying to hand us an umbrella. Or the man walking directly toward me.

"Audrey," Officer Mike rips my hands away from Dee, spins me around, and places my hands behind my back. "You're under arrest for the murder of Mallory—"

"No!" I try to jerk my hands from his, but he tightens his hold and quickly cuffs me before I get a chance to break away.

"You're lucky I didn't make it inside to do this where everyone could see. Let's not make this into a bigger scene."

I yell at Dee to remember what I said and nod her toward the carriage, but I'm turned around before I get a chance to ensure she makes it.

"I didn't kill Mallory or those girls." My arms start to burn as he jerks me forward.

"Audrey," he warns.

I can't fight this, not without causing a scene and making a fool out of myself or the girls. I am beyond lucky no one else is outside to witness this, except for the few guards by the door and maybe a few footmen.

SINISTER DESIRE

The clock tower chimes, announcing an hour till midnight. I still had an hour.

I knew this was never about money. They wanted me at the ball so they could somehow frame me for the murders in front of everyone. They expected I would either be caught in the midst of stealing or in my harlot ways, making an even bigger spectacle of myself.

As Mike pushes me forward roughly, a flash of white catches my eye, but when I look up no one is there.

Chapter Sixteen

"You were seen following after the guard and running into the harlot who was found dead the other day, and you were the last one seen with Mallory. You're in possession of their jewelry, Mallory's ring!" Mike glares at me from across the table, a table covered in my stalker's notes, bookmarks, and jewelry I recognize from Ember's jewelry box.

He points his chin toward me, eyeing my necklace. "You have a thing for emeralds? Couldn't wait to take Mallory's, could you?"

I shake my head, half in disbelief and the other to emphasize my point. "Ember is framing me."

"Why would she want to frame you? Her own stepmother?" If sarcasm had a look, it's the one he's giving me right now. He's already made up his mind that I'm the murderer.

"I don't know," I answer honestly. I don't know why the psychopath does what she does. I've let my own past cloud my judgments of her and blind me to what was right in front of me. "She wanted her dowry money and the house." I'm scrambling to find any reason Ember would murder those girls and try to frame me.

"I spoke with Ember." Mike sits back in his chair, twisting his mustache between his fingers. The movement ignites a rage in me while I remain handcuffed as if I'm a danger to him. "She believes *you* caused Richard's accident."

SINISTER DESIRE

My throat dries. I never saved those notes. There is absolutely no way she knows I poisoned him.

"I don't think you murdered your husband, but she brought up some other interesting points. Like how you manage to provide for yourself and those girls even without an inheritance or any form of income, how you were able to swing not one, but four tickets to the prince's ball tonight." He leans forward like he's just won a game. "I know you're a harlot, and I think you killed those girls so you can take their clients."

His theory is wrong but even I can't deny it's perfect. With the evidence separating us on this table, I don't have an argument or a plea, just racing thoughts. All hope diminishes as he leans back in his chair, takes out his cigarette, and lights it without a worry in the world. He thinks he caught the harlot killer.

"Why would you buy your girls new dresses but make Ember wear that old wedding dress?"

"She chose to wear it without my knowledge or approval," I grit through my teeth.

"Ah," he nods, convincing himself that I'm lying. "I was there at their ceremony, you know?"

I shake my head, not believing what I'm hearing. Part of me thought she was bluffing when she showed me those rings, but a ceremony?

"They stopped here and asked if I would be a witness because neither of them had any family they wanted present. Said she's scared of you. That you lock her in the attic with the rats, refuse to let anyone court her because you're scared she'll tell everyone what really goes on in that house. Her uncle Jack even confirmed that he found rat meat in the soup the other day." He shakes his head, disgusted. "Those two married so they could claim the house to finally be rid of you."

CRUEL KINGDOMS

I don't say anything. I can't. The girl has frighteningly baffled me this time, and I don't have a leg to stand on.

Mike stands from his chair, puts out his cigarette, and rounds the table, leaning against it so close that I can smell the alcohol lingering in his clothes. "I liked you, Audrey. I really did. I felt horrible after Robert died and you were left alone with those girls, and I thought it was commendable that you looked after Ember like your own. It's just a shame I didn't really know you at all."

"Mike, please, I swear I didn't murder those women."

"I want to believe you." The way he's sitting allows him to look down at me—to intimidate me. But men like him don't. The smell of the whiskey on his clothes does, but he doesn't. "Even if I ignore Ember's claims and we say she's just a disgruntled stepdaughter, and I ignored the fact that you had the victim's jewelry hidden away in a locked box, I can't ignore the poison growing in your garden where, as Ember and your twins confirmed, you've been visiting more frequently. It's consistent with what was used on the victims to incapacitate them."

My head is spinning. Ember… "Gus is my groundskeeper. He's out there once a month, and Ember lives with me. You can't pin all of this on me without looking at them too!"

"Gus was fired a year ago, and Ember has alibis for the time of the deaths. Unfortunately for you, I have a feeling your alibis won't be so forthcoming."

Of course not. None of those men will admit to hiring a harlot. But I know that's what I was doing during every one of those deaths. With my gut telling me this was Ember and Gus, I have a feeling they've been planning this for a while. I just don't know why.

SINISTER DESIRE

"Can you please send someone to check on my girls?" I stare at him with pleading in my eyes. "I'll tell you whatever you want. I'll—"

The door burst open. The frame cracks and the entire thing falls to the floor.

Charming doesn't have to search for me. He clocks me the moment he steps through, his dark eyes wild, slanting, when he sees how close Mike is to me.

In two strides, he grabs Mike by his collar and slams him against the wall. I'm too mesmerized by him to look away or try to stand. He holds Mike's throat and lifts, turning his face purple and making his feet dangle, struggling to stay connected to the floor.

"*Mike*," he sneers his name like a curse. "Who gave you permission to cuff her?"

Mike tries to speak but struggles for the simplest of breaths. Charming turns his head. "I can't hear you, Mike. Did you say this was an honest mistake?" With his head angled away, he notices the table and everything on it, eyes me, and realizes why exactly I'm here. "I was with Audrey during every murder that occurred."

Mike drops to the floor, gasping for air while Charming circles behind me to release the cuffs around my wrists. I don't understand how he's here or why Mike looks terrified, but I've never been more grateful. "You can't—" Mike huffs, struggling to regain control of himself.

"I can," Charming says it like it's an order. "Get him out of my sight. He reeks of alcohol. Relieve him of his duties immediately." Two men I didn't notice, dressed as palace guards, lift a disgruntled Mike and drag him out of the room.

CRUEL KINGDOMS

When Charming looks back at me, his eyes hold a shade of softness with the damning fury still radiating from him. "Did he hurt you?" I rub my wrists where they're red and raw. "*Little bird?*"

I snap my head up and nod, confusion clouding my mind. "I'm fine. We have to go." There isn't time to worry or talk about what just happened. My stalker has power, that's all I know, and he knows the danger Ally is in. We're out the door before I can take another breath.

This time, when the question arises, I give it a voice. He might be my stalker, but he was nowhere near me when I was arrested. "How did you know I was here?" I ask as he helps me on the horse. He lifts himself to settle behind me, and we take off.

"Dove saw him take you."

"I knew she wasn't blind." That woman sees more than anyone else I know.

I feel him smirk behind me, but he neither confirms nor denies it. "Delany is safe with her friends. My guy is headed to the house for Ally."

That was one relief I needed to hear. Dee was okay. No matter what happens, Dee would be fine.

Neither of us talk any further. I'm too lost in my head, filled with too many questions and trying to battle away the horrific possibilities I hope we're not about to walk into.

Charming told me he sent guards to the house, but as we arrive, no one is here but a single horse. I jump from ours and run toward the door, but he stops me and insists I stay outside. They're expecting me, not him.

No amount of words can describe the dreaded terror I feel watching him sneak around the house and disappear through a window. He lifted himself and leaps through with such practiced precision that I'm reminded he's done this many times before.

I don't hear or see anything from where I wait by the back gardens. All I can do is pace with my eyes darting in every corner of the massive home. Again, I find it too much now. There are too many windows, too many stories, and the way the night sky barely graces it with light it's far too decrepit.

Where is he?

If I trust anyone to help Ally, it's my stalker... *Charming*. He's controlled, quiet, and willing to kill.

A sharp scream pierces the air—I'm running.

I don't care if they know I'm coming. I don't care about anything right now as I burst through the back door. The sight I find stalls me for a fraction of a second before I'm moving again.

A man in a beast mask looks to me from where he's stalking Jack around the dining table. There is nothing appealing about his mask, only dread and a tremor of fear pulls from me at the sight.

Both are holding knives, but my bets are on the beast, who's back to eyeing Jack with a predatory snarl. This must be the guy Charming was talking about.

I continue through the house, screaming Ally's name. There isn't one room I don't check. They're all empty. All but one.

I rush down the upstairs hall and reach for my keys, but I don't need them. The door to the attic is wide open.

There's not a chance of walking up these steps quietly. Too many times, I've heard Richard's approach when he finally came to release me from my prison. Once a sound that brought me relieved freedom is now the sound that's taunting me, each creak and worn whimper whispering it's too late.

By the time I'm rounding the banister, they're waiting for me.

Light struggles to seep through the lone window Ember is looking out of, sitting on the edge and swinging her leg. Everything is given a red hue from the stained glass above. If I didn't know any better, she'd look like a lost girl pondering her life and praying to the moon.

My sole attention isn't on this girl, but on Ally, where she's tied to a chair with her mouth gagged and Gus hovering behind her with a knife to her throat. Charming, lying at his feet with blood pooling around him.

Not again.

"You have everything. The house is yours. What more do you want?" My voice croaks. I'm not sure who I'm asking this question to. Was it Gus who convinced Ember or was all of this her idea?

I get my answer when Ember speaks first.

"Did you know if this home burns, there is insurance?" Ember slides her snakelike gaze toward me. "That was one of the first ways I imagined killing you all." Her face falls into a panic as she grips her chest and wipes her cheeks "My poor family was burned in a fire officer. I tried… I really did, but I couldn't get them out." She collects herself and continues, "I'd then be given the money, and life is as it should be. But then I realized that wouldn't be very fun. You're all dead, and then what? I marry, move on, and have children?" Her face contorts into a sick gag. "If these last few years taught me anything, it's that I like playing with people."

When she pauses, I chance a look back at her again. She's irritated now and eyeing Ally. Her chin dips, motioning toward Gus, who drops the knife against Ally's throat and stalks toward me.

SINISTER DESIRE

I'm too panicked to do anything but let him wrap his arms around my entire body and drag me toward the pile of broken glass in the corner.

Ember leaves her windowsill to stand inches from me. Her icy blue eyes are a mirror to the cold heart she holds. "Lift your dress and kneel."

"Why?"

Her shoulders lift and drop. "I want you to. It's easier to talk when I know you're not thinking of ways to save your daughter." The knife passes by my face as Gus hands it to her. She takes a step back in the direction of Ally and gives me the ultimatum of dropping to my knees or killing my daughter.

No matter how slow or fast, this is going to hurt. I don't bother contemplating which is better or worse as I fall to my knees and clench my teeth so tight I think they'll shatter. Glass pierces my skin. A cold, hot, searing pain rips into me, sending my entire body into a rattling shiver.

Gus' massive hands grip my shoulders to push me down. I cry out.

Ember lets out a maniacal laugh that lifts my head. "You have no idea how long this took to plan. After I followed you that day and confirmed you were whoring yourself out, everything fell into place too easily. Gus told me about the poisonous plants. I tested them out, of course. Lucy didn't even know she ingested them before climbing that tree, but Brock had his suspicions. I guess I couldn't hold my laugh in when she fell and broke her arm." *Oops,* she mouths. "The other whores were much easier. And *so* much more enjoyable than those rats. The only part that didn't go as planned was the ball. You were supposed to be whoring or stealing when Mike arrested you before dragging you through the ball in cuffs." She's back at me, pointing the knife to my throat. "It would have been so perfect. And I would visit you behind bars to tell you how profitable your daughters are."

"Why?" I yell. "I cared for you as if you were my own!"

CRUEL KINGDOMS

"I had a mother!" Spit flies from her mouth as the knife pinches my neck hard enough to draw blood. "And you ruined her. When she found out about you, she was different. And so was he. We knew every time he left, it was to be with you. My mother doted on him every second of every day after that. It was the day she ran after him in the cold, begging for him to stay, that she got sick. Because he left us to go to *you!*"

Her words don't mean anything to me. I spent too much of my time trying to understand and give this girl excuses to be cruel. I just needed her distracted to get what I needed.

I tighten my fist around the large shard in my hand, bend my head away from the knife, and bring the glass down into Gus' calf.

I get one foot to the ground when Ember swings the knife back at me. I catch her wrist and pull her into me. We both fall back, taking Gus to the ground behind us. Glass pierces our bodies as our cries fill the attic.

Ember squirms away and kicks my stomach, crawling toward the fallen knife. My focus isn't on her, though. Not as Gus' groans become more alert.

He jumps up, eyeing me with pure hatred. He takes one step before someone knocks him down. The man with the beast mask straddles him, pulling a knife from behind his back.

Neither of us saw the match in Gus' hand until he drops it onto the old fabric. Within seconds, the pile ignites as the knife comes down on his neck.

"You—" Ember starts. I'm tackled to the ground, quickly turning onto my back just in time to see the glistening above my head. Ember brings the knife down. I dodge my head just in time.

My fist meets her cheek, but hers hits mine right back.

SINISTER DESIRE

"Why did you have to take him from us?!"

As the knife comes down, I grab her hand, holding it inches from my face. She leans forward, and with the added pressure, I turn my head, letting the blade slice my cheek.

She leans in with a smile I want to wipe clean off, "I'm going to take him from you!" Her weight is off me within a second, stumbling to her feet as she runs toward Charming.

Ally is gone from the chair. I look around and find the beast helping her toward the window, the fire growing wildly behind them.

With Ally safe, I use everything left inside of me to tackle Ember to the ground, sending us tipping over Charming.

I re-grip the knife, push all my weight into rolling us over, and feel the moment the knife punctures her. It's as if time stops.

"No, no…" I grab Ember's face, trying to keep her eyes from rolling back. "No, you're okay." Her head falls back, and I swear I see the life leave her body. "I'm sorry. I'm so, so, sorry."

"Mom, we have to go." I hear Ally yelling at me, but I'm too in shock at the lifeless eyes before me. I thought I'd seen a dead body before, but staring into Ember's lifeless eyes is different. The void in them opens one inside me.

I feel hands pull at my shoulders, calling for me, but I can't move. Smoke fills the air, and I can't even cough.

I don't know how he removes my hands from her, but somehow Ember is gone from them, and I'm in Charming's arms. I feel like I'm outside of my body, watching Ally on the beast's back, carefully climbing out of the window and disappearing down it. I hope she doesn't break another leg.

CRUEL KINGDOMS

Charming is telling me something, but I can't hear anything. It's the void Ember's death filled in me. I know he curses and ties something around us to keep me secured to him as he climbs us out the window and down the ladder. I'm not making it easy for him, but he manages to bring us to the ground and keep me in his arms.

It's not until I see Ally hug Dee that breath fills my lungs again, and the noise around me returns. They're safe.

Charming is nodding his head, repeating my thoughts out loud. He's covered in blood, claiming it's just a scratch, that he was down because Gus snuck up behind him and knocked him out.

A guard approaches us. "The King forbade us from coming. I couldn't leave until the ball started to die down. On my honor, I'm truly sorry. We'll deal with this." He nods toward Charming. "What's the *official* story?"

"Fired groundskeeper returns to the house for revenge. Kills the harlot serial killer in the process." Charming says quickly and swiftly. I listen in silence, too focused on the authority in his voice. "These three are with me now. Ensure they're treated as family. You understand?"

"Of course, prince." The guard nods and walks off.

"Prince?!" I balk at him. My stalker is not a prince.

He lets out a breath that mimics a chuckle, walking us to a bench as the property swarms with guards. Useless guards.

"You'll be fine." He's looking at my knee and starts pulling glass like I'm going to die if he doesn't get every piece out. I would help him, but I'm too busy waiting for him to explain.

"Are you going to explain why that man called you prince?"

SINISTER DESIRE

"Do you really not know?" He looks me over like I'm lying.

"Apparently not. I saw the prince. He danced with Ember."

He leans in and lowers his voice. "It's a safety precaution. We rule from behind the pretty face we show the public."

"Don't worry, they pay them handsomely for it." The man in the beast mask stands before us.

"This is Duke. He's a friend." Charming explains.

"Friend is a weak word for someone who just saved your daughter's life."

Charming's head snaps toward him before pulling a knife from behind his back and threatening between his legs. "You talk too much."

My mouth drops. "You know?!"

"How could he not? The one with black hair is his fucking twin. And the one with red hair was talking about how she's in love with me for saving her life. If she's anything like him, I'm in for a lifetime of stalking."

Charming presses the knife in harder, his eyes threatening without the words needing to be said. "I've never heard you talk so much in your life. If you don't stop, I'm going make sure you never do."

Duke chuckles, holding his hands in defense. "Must be all of the adrenaline." He turns and walks off with that same strong gait Charming has. "I'll leave you to it, *prince*," he calls back.

That word again. I don't believe it. Any of it.

"If you're really the prince, then your father is—"

CRUEL KINGDOMS

"Dead to me." His face turns cold and stoic. "But yes, he is the King—not the face, you know. After I spoke with you tonight, I found him, and he confirmed that he paid your father to keep the twins a secret and paid Richard to claim them as his. He gave my necklace to your father to make my death look convincing to you, so you'd never try to find the father of your children."

My heart splinters. Knowing this doesn't change what happened or how we got here, but it hurts to know our lives were ripped from us by a selfish man, and while I made the best of the situation I was given, the larger part of me grieves for the life we all could have had.

He takes my head into his hand and makes me look at him as he tells me, "You did everything for them. Never think twice about it. You told me long ago, *'It could always be worse,'* and it's those bleakly optimistic words that kept me sane all these years. Remember them now. You did what you had to do when you were running from your father, when you raised our girls, and when you *stopped* Ember."

The last words strike me like the knife I used to kill her.

"Everything could have been so much worse." His eyes ask the question of understanding, and I nod. If I hadn't killed Ember, she would have killed Ally or worse.

"What now?"

"You'll stay with me. Duke and Dove live there part-time, but they won't be a bother. It's a smaller palace but big enough for all of us and some. You won't ever have to worry about my father." The smile that lifts on his face gives me pause. One that has me waiting for him to finish before I decide if I should be scared or not. "I gave him the papers that I filled out the second I confirmed you were alive. He knows if anything happens to you or the girls, I resign my royal line, and if anything happens to me, it all goes to you."

SINISTER DESIRE

"Why the ball?"

I wince as he pulls another piece of glass from my leg. "Because when I marry, the face prince has to, too."

"Charming," I have arguments on the tip of my tongue, but he speaks before I get a word out.

"Cain." I look at him, confused. "That's my real name, Cain Aramos. Officially, anyway." He lifts me again, heading toward the carriage. "But to you, it's always Charming, little bird."

Epilogue: Cain

One Year Later

My little bird is back. That smile she likes to give the world, the one that looks genuine but is pulled higher by the invisible strings of drunken fists and forced bravery, is more authentic with every passing day.

She's more beautiful than the day I found her covered in dirt and blood, hiding by the pumpkins. It was that smile that lifted on her tear-streaked face, greeting me before her breathing turned to chokes. I don't even think she knew blood coated her lips. There was something about her—about *that* smile—she was like a wounded bird I wanted to mend back together.

So, I did.

By the time I got her to my room, she was barely breathing. My sister had an allergic reaction before; I knew exactly how to help. By the time her breathing eased, I cleaned her up myself and stitched the cut on her back.

When she didn't wake right away, I grew worried. By the second day, I swore to her that if she died, I'd follow her straight to Hell because only the devil would send a gift to me only to take her away too soon. Nothing and no one would keep me from my little bird, not even death.

I was on the verge of being desperate enough to seek the help of my father, something I'd never done in my life, but she woke up.

SINISTER DESIRE

I knew then that I was going to keep her as mine forever. And I promised her that she would feel the same fear I felt when I thought she was about to die. It wasn't fair for her to make me feel that way.

A prince isn't allowed friends, especially not a girl. He is supposed to marry for land and money, to strengthen the kingdom. His friends are his guards and neighboring royals.

But she was mine.

No one ever stopped by; I was too on point with my schedule. No one needed to wake me or kiss me to bed. Not even my sisters were around to bother us—off in neighboring towns, schmoozing the other royals and preparing their marriage requests. At least our father lets them have a semblance of choosing their own partners.

Those days with her felt like years passed and went by in the blink of an eye at the same time. Neither of us talked about our lives right away, just her wants and my desires. I get everything I want, so hearing hers was different. She had hope and loss in her voice as she spoke about them, with that damn smile. So sorrowful and yet so full of promise.

She never asked who I was, and I never told her I was the prince. I didn't want her to look at me differently because of it. My rooms were lavish and looked enough like a normal home for her to question it. We stayed in my rooms for days, playing games and leaving notes to throw the other off course. Not just hiding from the rest of the world but forgetting about it altogether.

It was after every scare when I jumped out of my hiding spots or grabbed her from hers, peeking over her shoulder when I chased her around, that her smile grew more genuine. The flush in her cheeks told me everything I needed to know—my little bird liked the thrill.

CRUEL KINGDOMS

It was the freshly baked bread that made her eyes glimmer before they closed to isolate that one sense to smell the cinnamon better. I brought it back for all meals. Rosemary at dinner and cinnamon at breakfast.

By the last night, she finally told me how she got the cut on her back. How her father was abusive toward her mother until she died, and his fists started toward her. The night she ran away, that fist was a knife. I made her show me again, and when I saw it, I couldn't stop myself—couldn't stop her.

I couldn't stop at just the kiss, and neither could she. We were each other's firsts and couldn't keep our hands off each other the rest of the night.

The next morning, I missed my training, and she was being carried away by guards.

I ran after them until more guards showed up and stopped me. At my father's order, they held me down and forced me to watch them take her back to that hell she escaped from. The one I promised she would never have to go back to as long as she stayed in my room.

That was the day my own hell began. The misery and mundane life that I was promised. I wasn't going to play by the King's rules, though. As long as I served the country, I wouldn't be forced to marry until I returned.

During my time away serving, I met Duke, who brought me into The Trove and introduced me to Dove, whose specialty is finding the unfindable. They were the ones who made me realize how blind I was for taking my father's word and a tombstone as facts that she was dead.

When Dove sent me that clipping of Audrey, I had to spar with Duke for nearly two days straight to keep myself from killing my father.

She'd been in our Kingdom all this time. Right under my fucking nose, my little bird was, in fact, alive, married, and had children. I knew immediately they were mine. Richard was blonde with blue eyes. Dee, the raven-haired girl, was practically my twin, while Ally was Audrey's, except for my dimples and the auburn hair.

I want to say I don't care what she did to survive, to give our twins a life, but that would be a lie. I fucking hated it. Could I have barged into her life and uprooted her? *No.* I didn't know her anymore. I had to bide my time and watch from afar—plan.

My wife lies in our bed now, in our home that's far away from the prison she lived in for too long and even farther from my father. He's still one man I can't kill—yet.

Her dark hair splays over the silk pillow. Her back is to me and I'm instantly hard seeing my initial between her shoulder blades. My royal insignia. Any guard or royal who sees it knows she's mine and to protect her at all costs. The knotted swirl at the end of the C might look fancy to any normal eye but holds a specific meaning to anyone in The Trove to do the same.

As for the ones who worked the harlot operation, we still don't know who they are. They disappeared after seeing Audrey's back and haven't been back since.

I wrap my arm around my wife's waist. She whimpers, complaining she's too sore to go at it again. I chuckle against her neck, remembering why she's sore at all.

While she didn't want to belong to anyone again, she had no objections when I chased her in the woods outside of our home, slid the diamond on her finger—because emeralds only reminded her of death now—and told her she was mine. She doesn't need to know that we've been legally married since the day her husband died.

I get what I desire.

CRUEL KINGDOMS

Which brings me back to why she's sore. The ceremony last night was small, but my father insisted on having a reception filled with other royals. It's tradition and, as he pointed out, allows for my sisters and the girls to mingle with other royals and build those connections, so we placated him.

It was when a princess from another kingdom touched my hand a little longer than polite that I saw the moment of understanding fill my little bird's glower. She never asked me why I killed the dollmaker or doctor, and she doesn't know about the rest of them, the ones she put such a show on for when she thought I was watching, but it was at that moment she knew exactly why—someone's touching her things.

I picked her up over my shoulder, in the white dress she made herself, and took her home, spending the rest of the night showing her who I belonged to.

There was one thing she didn't know, something she would have to ask me directly, and if she did, I would be forced to answer. I would never lie to my sweet little bird.

All she has to ask is if I killed her husband. I would be forced to answer honestly. Yes.

I would have to admit that when I came back after seeing the photo of her, I came to her house to take her back with me. I didn't care if I had to take her kicking and screaming. I would tell her that I saw her sad in the attic window, no faux smile on her face, just sorrow as she watched the girls laughing and playing outside.

That's when I realized I had to wait and watch. She was a shell of the girl I knew and shells crack when they're rattled too hard.

I left the first note that day, promising her freedom, knowing I would do everything in my power to ensure it.

SINISTER DESIRE

If she did ask about killing her husband, I would also have to admit that I didn't actually give her poison to murder him, just something that would dye his lips blue that told me she was willing enough to do it.

I planted Dove and Duke as a new couple in town to ensure Richard was distracted if and when Audrey decided to poison him herself. It had been a long time since a genuine smile lifted on my face, and the moment Richard found me waiting for him in his carriage, with his wide eyes and blue lips, I couldn't stop myself from grinning like a child. I strangled him, cut his horse loose, and pushed his carriage over the cliff.

He was always meant to die at my hands for touching her with his.

It was that day Audrey took a stand in her life, and I won't take that away from her by telling her the truth unless she asks me.

When I learned Richard drained his bank accounts and planned to leave them all behind for a new woman, leaving them with nothing, I tried to send Audrey gifts and money, but she wouldn't take them. I couldn't show up and tell her everything either. I still had a year to spend in the military before my time was up. I had Dove watch her at a distance as I sent the notes and gifts for her to leave for me.

We told the girls a very condensed version of our lives, and Ally called me their fairy godmother.

More like an avenging angel.

Duke was right, she takes after me, always lurking in the shadows, pining after him without even trying to hide it. The self-assurance in that girl is unmatched by anyone I've ever met. Dee, on the other hand, may look just like me, but is all Audrey: the glowers, subtle defiance, and the same smile that reveals their dream for more. Not material things either, neither of them are impressed by it, not like Ally, who wore a diadem for a week straight after learning she is a princess.

CRUEL KINGDOMS

He might not admit it, but Duke's been agitated with Dove gone, pulling me away from my wife to spar with him so he doesn't do something stupid. I would ignore him if he hadn't helped me more times than I can count.

It could be where Dove went that has him on edge. The neighboring Kingdom isn't known for being welcoming, and the fact that it's where my sister Eva's getting her revenge should say enough about it.

It could also be the fact that Mel is with them. She could fuck off since she tried to sleep with my wife, but I swear she's cursed, and I really don't want the other two to suffer because of it.

Shit, there are two things Audrey would need to ask. Did I kill her father? Yes. I came back within a year after our fathers split us up. I found him drunk at a bar, hitting on a girl young enough to be his daughter.

Mel, as much as I don't like interacting with her, happened to have a poison that mimics heart attacks. I still owe her for it.

It was killing him that flashed through my head when I joined Duke and The Trove. Even though I thought Audrey was dead, it felt too damn good to rid the world of a man like him. A man who looks like any other on the outside but secretly abuses his wife and daughter, a man who gets off on the power.

Aside from being a prince, killing the corrupted is what I live to do, my purpose, and it's all thanks to her.

As for the King, my father, he's forced to accept Audrey and the twins as his family. All the paperwork now lists me as their father, including their birth certificates. It's the false prince who was forced to wed and adopt two children to mimic our lives. The man is paid enough not to care.

Ember's body was never found and never will be. She's burned to a crisp and rotting deep in the ground with Gus, Jack, and the rest of the

SINISTER DESIRE

sorry fucks who found their lives twisted into ours. One of the most recent ones is the dressmaker who turned Audrey away for being a harlot. The shop is now hers, and though she doesn't have to work, she's brilliant with a needle, and I can't deny what she wants.

My wife groans next to me as I slide into her. "Charming?"

"Yes, little bird?"

Anything.

CRUEL KINGDOMS

Little Bird

Sixteen Years Ago

My feet ache and sting from running for so long. The sun was still high in the sky when I started, but I'm surrounded by the midnight moon that offers little light to my surroundings—grass. Miles of it, except for a tall wall in the distance.

I shouldn't have run so far, but with every step, my back sang for me to keep going. To get as far away from my father as possible.

I can't go back.

I'll die if I go back. Just like my mother.

I suck in a wheezy breath, sweat tickling my temples and soaking my dress as I approach the looming stone wall. I need to get on the other side. Something else to create an even greater distance from him.

As if hearing my prayers, I see a crumbled opening and crawl through it perfectly. It's as if someone carved it out just for me.

When I break the other side, my labored breath is caught at the sight of the largest garden I've seen yet. Apple trees, lemon trees, roses, peonies, perfectly sculpted hedges, pumpkins.

I might be imagining this glorious landscape with how dizzy I've become all of a sudden.

SINISTER DESIRE

It's the pumpkin patch I find first, stumbling toward it with uneven footing. My head grows fuzzy the closer I get. My hands land on one of them, slipping on its round edge and planting me straight into the cool dirt.

Oh, God.

I try to breathe, but every breath is increasingly more difficult than the last.

"Who are you?"

My head snaps toward the unfamiliar voice. The sight I'm met with puts everything into perspective.

My father actually did it this time, or maybe it was me with how long I ran without stopping to tend to the cut on my back, but there isn't a doubt in my mind that I'm dying.

The angel before me is out of a dream except for the hardness in his stone-set features and the coldness in his eyes. If this is hell, it's much better than home already.

I can't help but smile as the world darkens around me.

My eyes open, adjusting to the soft light around me.

I've never known comfort or warmth like I do now. The covers on me are black furs and the softest material I've ever had the blessing of touching, let alone being wrapped in.

I don't get to take in anything else when I feel eyes on me.

CRUEL KINGDOMS

It's the boy again, the beautiful demon from the garden. He's sitting on a chair next to the bed, his hands in the pockets of his pants, and he's holding the same icy stare, only it's even colder now, with his jaw twitching as if he's angry.

"Who hurt you?"

My back tingles as if all the pain was being held by this boy and he returned it with his assertive voice. I sit up, wincing as the sting begins to throb.

He's waiting, but I don't offer him anything. I can't. If I'm really not dead, then I can't admit anything. No one can know about my father. I made the mistake of trying to confide in someone once, anything to stop him from hitting my mother, and that error in judgment left her unable to walk for a week.

Instead, I twist my head, taking in the extravagant room, and ask, "Where am I?"

"Better than where you were." He looks me over, assessing—judging—my too-thin figure, my…

Nightgown?

"Did you change me?!" I toss the furs off and see that I am indeed in only a nightgown that cuts off above the knee. Quickly, I pull the furs back up, heightening them to my neck. "Where in the hell am I?"

"My home." He offers no warmth in his answer. "I cleaned you up, changed you, and…" he looks up like he can't recall something and then points as if suddenly remembering, "Oh right, I saved your life."

My cheeks heat at the thought of him seeing me naked.

"Don't worry. This cage is big enough for both of us."

SINISTER DESIRE

"Both of us?" This time, I don't care that the furs aren't covering me when they fall to my waist. He can't mean to keep me here?

He rises from his chair, brushing his black hair back with his hand before walking to the other side of the room that's larger than my entire house. "You're underfed, you were obviously attacked, and you broke into my garden to die. Do you want to leave here, where I can feed you the best food and keep you safe?"

When he puts it like that... My eyes narrow on him. "What do you want?"

The entire world stops to give him time to lift his crooked grin, revealing perfect white teeth, one a little too sharp. "I don't *want* anything." He pauses, leaning himself against a desk and twirling the necklace around his neck between his fingers. "But I will ensure you know exactly what it felt like watching you die for two days."

My head is working to understand what he could mean, but the dark promise written on his face does something to me that I didn't expect. I gulp, suddenly aware of my need for water.

"I'll give you until the count of thirty to hide."

My hand covers my mouth to hide my breathing, which should be quiet but is somehow louder than ever. My traitorous heart is there with it, penetrating the air as if screaming for him to find me hidden in the closet.

Through the crack, I see him walk by. My back leans against the wall, silently praying for the shadows to hide me into them.

"We know how this is going to end, Audrey."

CRUEL KINGDOMS

I can no longer see or hear him now. My blood is pumping, waiting for the inevitable. The spike in my heart widens my eyes to be more alert.

Leaning closer to the crack, I still don't see anything.

The door burst open.

My scream is caught in my palm as I jump to my feet. There is no way out except through him.

His head cocks.

The deepening smirk on his face only makes me aware of the one I'm giving him. "Don't even think about it."

I lunge toward him, sending us both back out of the closet. His hand wraps around my back as he falls to his, pulling me with him.

I can't stop myself from bursting with laughter before I shoot back to my feet and run toward the dining room, our cinnamon bread still on the table from when he interrupted us with 'The King says it's time for a game.

His footsteps are close behind, gaining on me with every second. I round the table and dart back to the room. I'm not two steps in before his arms wrap around my waist and he's tossing me onto the bed.

"Got you," he boasts before turning me over to check the stitches.

It's been three days of this. Hiding, running, and playing childish games before he leaves and comes back with the best food I've ever had. Sometimes he's gone too long, leaving me bored out of my mind, but he gave me ink and paper to write notes with hints about where I'm hiding for him—none of which are accurate.

Once he's finished looking me over, he asks a question like always. I haven't won as many games, so I hardly know anything about him, not even his name. Charming is what I call him because he was so detestable that first day, and it made him smile for the first time when I used it—a real smile, not the amused one he always gives me.

His fingers trace my spine, circling the long cut down my back. "How did you get this?"

By now he knows nearly everything about me, but that is one thing he doesn't.

I flip over so we're sitting side by side, our knees brushing as I wring my hands together. They're sweating all of a sudden.

With his finger, he lifts my chin to meet his stony glare, the one he hasn't used at all these last few days. "We have a deal. Whoever wins gets to ask any question, and the other must answer honestly."

"I know." I swallow, trying to will the words out before I'm too scared to speak again. It's not like I'm ever going back there, so I'm not sure why it's so hard to admit.

When his hand presses against my back, I exhale. "It was my father. He… it used to just be my mother. She'd tell me to run until it was over. I'd find a garden and wait it out. After she died, though, he started to hit me. This day, I guess I was eating too loud while he was cutting his strawberries and… well, you saw it." I take another deep breath and repeat the mantra I've believed my entire life. "It could be worse."

He gives me the same face he did when I first said that phrase. One I can't decipher from amusement or astonishment. "It could also be better." His smile ticks to the side. "Strawberries?"

I nod.

His jaw ticks. "You're never going back there."

CRUEL KINGDOMS

I can't help but smile. Every day, he reminds me that I'm not going anywhere, that this is my home as much as it is his. The only rule is I can't leave, but he promises it'll only be a year until we can leave and be free—both of us, though I still don't know what he needs to be free of. I've been waiting to win a game to ask him.

Something passes between us. I don't know if it's the adrenaline from hiding and running or telling him about the abuse, but when his eyes fall to my lips, I don't hesitate to lean in and kiss him. He could turn me down, push me away, yell at me, I don't care. He always asks me what I want but it's more than that. I don't just want to kiss him, I need to.

The moment my lips meet his, his hands are on me, pulling me closer so I'm flush against him. He must want this as much as I do because his mouth leads mine open, his tongue brushing against mine.

I may have started this, but he's the one in control now. With the way my body is melted into him, I can't even think straight.

I'm not sure where to put my hands, and I don't get a chance to consider where before he leans me back.

He doesn't stop kissing, and neither do I. Only when he lifts his shirt over his head do we pause to let the fabric pass before we're back together.

My stomach flutters feeling him beneath my hands. I've seen him shirtless in passing but feeling him is so much different. His skin is soft, but he's hard with growing muscle.

My dress slides down. It's awkward trying to move it down my body while lying down, but with his help, it's off within seconds, along with his pants. There isn't a piece of clothing between us except for the emerald around his neck.

SINISTER DESIRE

He pulls back onto his knees, looking down at me with the softest features I've seen him possess. My hands cover my breasts as I peek at him, my throat drying at the sight.

His brows pinch together. "We don't have to."

My mouth parts. "I… do you not want to?"

He lets out a deep chuckle that makes my insides flip over itself all over again. "Are you kidding? If there's anything I want, it's this. *You*."

I hesitate, but it's all the reassurance I need to lower my hands to the side and wait with bated breath as he finishes raking his gaze up my body.

"I think I finally understand why Lucifer would fall from the Heavens." He lowers himself so he's a breath away, "I'd damn myself too if it meant being able to look at you every day." He brushes my hair away from my face. "You're perfect, Audrey."

My eyes aren't open, and I feel hands on my body, pulling me into their arms. "Charming, I can't."

"Get her out of here. Now!" A harsh voice jolts me awake. It's not Charming's arms I'm in at all, but a man who looks like he wants to throw me off the roof rather than carry me out of the room.

"Audrey!" Charming jumps out of bed, but I can't see him when the man who's holding me turns the corner. I don't dare look at my surroundings. I don't look at anything except the door we just left.

Charming rushes out, darting straight for us before he's tackled by two more men in all black, both struggling to keep him pinned down.

CRUEL KINGDOMS

"If you fight, it'll only be worse for him." The man holding me warns. My fists unravel, knowing all too well the promise of punishment.

The man with the harsh voice walks from the room, but I don't get a good look at him before he's bending down and whispering something I can't hear into Charming's ear.

Charming's blazing eyes don't leave mine as I'm being carried off, wrapped in only a sheet with our broken promises repeating through my mind.

My eyes are too filled with tears to see anything clearly as this man loads me into the carriage. Everything starts to haze over with a cold chill as if winter had come early. He sits next to me in complete silence for what feels like hours until we come to a stop. With a turn of my head, I see the place I thought I'd never have to see again.

I chance a look at my escort, but he doesn't notice or care. "Please don't make me go back."

"Wouldn't have to if he didn't miss training."

"You don't even know me." I try. "You can just drop me off someplace else."

His eyes drift toward me before going back to the nothingness in front of him. "Your father reported you missing last night. Black hair, green eyes, name's Audrey."

My heart sinks to my stomach when he opens the door, dismissing me with a shake of his head.

"Why are we going to the cemetery?" I ask my father. It's not that I don't want to visit my mother's grave, it's just that he doesn't.

SINISTER DESIRE

The whisky bottle is half finished before we leave the house without any explanation as to why we're going to the cemetery in the middle of the night.

The walk isn't far, but my feet hurt from running away two days ago. It's been weeks since I was dragged out of Charming's house and dumped on my doorstep, nearly naked. The first week, I couldn't even walk out of the house from the beating my father gave me. There was no soothing soil or open air, just a cramped room with a broken mattress; no furs or bread, but I did have the sheet I left in, and a few crackers. If I close my eyes, I could imagine them soft and tasting like rosemary or cinnamon.

We're down a few rows of tombstones when my father jerks my hand in the opposite direction from my mother's.

I know not to ask any further questions unless I want a backhand as an answer.

The farther back we head, the worse the sunken feeling in the pit of my stomach grows. I don't know why he had me dress in my nicest dress and brush my hair if we aren't seeing my mother.

As we near a fresh grave site, I stumble back, seeing flames smothering something in the bottom of the pit.

My father grabs my arm and yanks me back up, dragging me to the edge of the hole. I can't even turn my head before he's gripping the sides of my face and yelling at me to look. "You think about running away from your home again this will be you. Do you understand?"

My body shakes as I'm forced to watch another human being burn to death before me. Bile rushes to the back of my throat as nausea overtakes my entire being.

CRUEL KINGDOMS

When my father lets go, I think it's over, but he keeps one grip tight on me to keep me from running away. Digging into his raggedy jeans, he pulls out something that has me turning back to the burned body to look at it closer. There's no way to tell if it's him, but I know it is. The world around me spins out of control. I don't know when I fall to my knees, but pain bursts from them as the pebbles stab through my thin dress and into my skin.

This can't be real. He can't be dead. My body convulses as my stomach empties itself over the grass.

My father tosses the emerald necklace next to me, but I can't even look at it. I can't take my eyes off the corpse.

I can't take it. I can't be in this world, continuing on in this mundane life any longer. Death is always going to follow me, taking away anyone I care about. The hope of finding Charming again is gone. I might as well meet him and my mother in the afterlife. It has to be better than this.

I lunge myself forward, but arms wrap around my shoulders before I can take the plunge below me. "Not so fast, girl. Wouldn't want to have to give back that money."

I don't hear him, but my ears do ring at the sound of crunching pebbles behind me from someone's approach footsteps. I fist the emerald and turn.

"Richard," my father greets him without earning one back.

The man before me looks down at me with a curl on his lips. "Up," he orders.

By the looks of him, he's likely a lord. His blond hair is slicked back. His blue eyes hold an arrogance about them that only comes from those with power and money, and his clothes are perfectly straight without a wrinkle in them. He even has cufflinks.

SINISTER DESIRE

I clutch the emerald in my palm and struggle to my feet. The pebbles embedded into my knees make it harder than it should.

The man before me, Richard, takes me in, assessing me as one would to pick out a dress for the day. "At least you're not hard on the eyes. Let's go."

"Go? Go where?"

He turns back to me with a look of amusement that makes my skin crawl.

"Home. You're mine. Bought and paid."

"What?" My father gives me a look that tells me to behave, but I'm too confused to listen. "Bought?"

Richard nods. "You can walk, or I can throw you over my shoulder, but either way, you'll be coming with me. Whether you want dinner tonight is up to you."

My lips seal tight at the arguments and questions I have for both men staring at me, waiting for me to dare another word. Taking in the stark differences between the two, my father in rugged clothes that could disintegrate any minute and this new man who looks clean and regal, I come to the conclusion that Richard can't be worse than my father. This could be the 'it could be better' Charming had talked about.

Without looking back at the corpse or my father, who is standing there like he had just been entitled lord with lands and a new wife, I tighten my hand around the emerald, lift my chin, and follow Richard to whatever new life awaits me.

"You'll be a lady, which means you'll need to act like it. Seeing that shithole you lived in, I doubt you have proper manners at all." Richard starts rambling as the carriage drives on. "You'll meet with teachers daily who will teach you to be a lady. A wife. You'll be expected to attend and host parties..." he continues on, but I'm not listening. All I can think about is Charming's burning body.

He's still talking as we arrive, and he walks me through the massive home. If I didn't know any better, I would have thought it was a palace. There's a kitchen with an island, a dining room, a living room, a hosting room, a servant's room, and too many bedrooms to count. None of it matters to me. The only thing I take any real pause to notice is the massive garden out back.

We're upstairs, walking the halls as he explains each room until we arrive at the last one. It's massive with a four-poster bed, a chandelier, a fireplace, and a washroom attached. It only reminds me of Charming's, though It's nothing compared to his.

A hand rests on my shoulder, startling me back to reality. "As for expectations here. I won't be around much, so the home will be yours. I'll expect you to keep your figure, and after you give birth, you'll be held to that same standard. The servants know what to feed you to ensure it."

Instinctively, my hands cradle my stomach as I turn to face him. He can't know I'm pregnant. I barely know, and only because I can't stop throwing up and my boobs are so sore, I cry when the water's too cold in my bath. Surely, he wouldn't buy someone he knows is carrying someone else's child.

Whether he knows or not, I look at him with real plea in my eyes. "Please never let my children see my father. I won't ask anything of you but that."

He gives me a curt nod and raises his hand back to my shoulder. Bile is at the back of my throat again when he kicks the door closed and tells me to go to the bed.

My hand finds the emerald around my neck.

SINISTER DESIRE

It's fine, I tell myself, *it's just Charming.*

ACKNOWLEDGMENTS

I am truly grateful for everyone who has helped bring this book to life. This novella came to be on a whim and spiraled into the idea of an entire series that I could not get out of my head.

My forever best friend, cousin, editor, soundboard, and all the other hats you wear, Geena, I am indebted to you for a lifetime for putting up with me.

As always, Nadia, you are the most patient person I know for letting me talk endlessly about the ideas that stick and don't stick. If you ever get a chance to read this, I am sorry for not warning you this was a dark romance.

My husband, Nick, you're never going to read this, but thank you for supporting me always.

Made in the USA
Columbia, SC
29 March 2025